MY LIFE AS
DINOSAUR
DENTAL FLOSS

Other My Life As... Books

a Smashed Burrito with Extra Hot Sauce

Alien Monster Bait

a Broken Bungee Cord

Crocodile Junk Food

Dinosaur Dental Floss

a Torpedo Test Target

For other books by Bill Myers, including more of the My Life As... series, stop by www.billmyers.com.

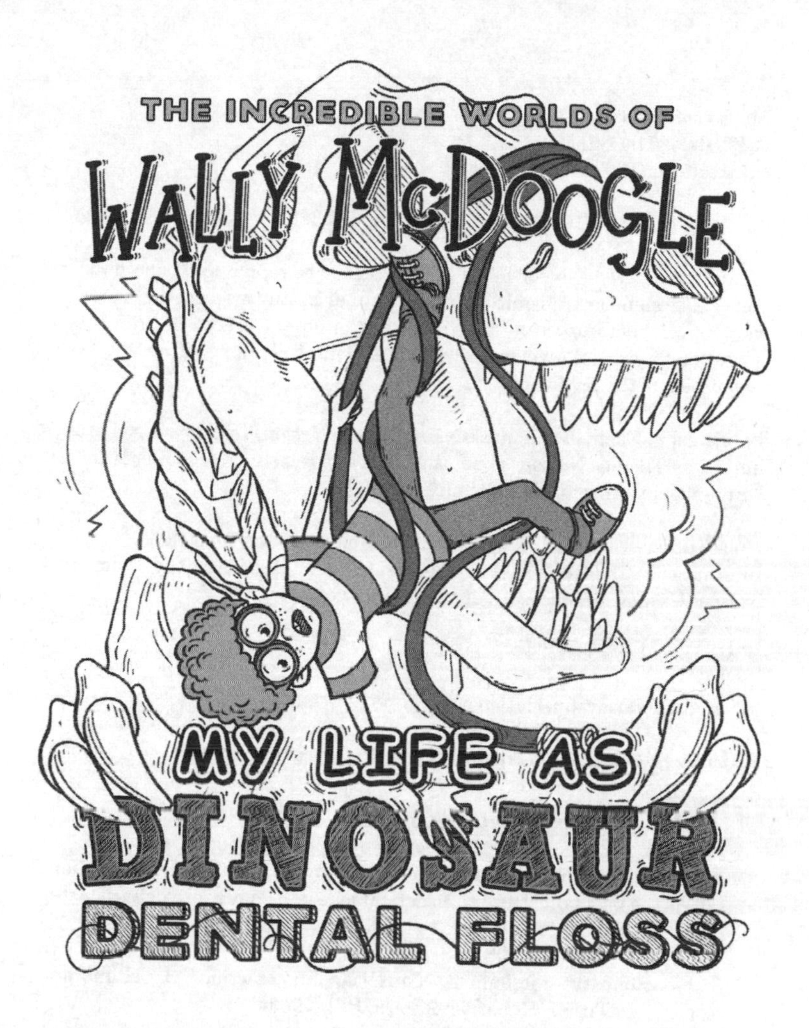

BILL MYERS

An Imprint of Thomas Nelson

My Life as Dinosaur Dental Floss

Tommy Nelson, PO Box 141000, Nashville, TN 37214

Published in Nashville, Tennessee, by Tommy Nelson. Tommy Nelson is an imprint of Thomas Nelson. Thomas Nelson is a registered trademark of HarperCollins Christian Publishing, Inc.

ISBN-13: 978-0-7852-3240-7

Cover and interior illustrations: Julianne St. Clair

Library of Congress Cataloging-in-Publication Data

Myers, Bill, 1953–
My life as dinosaur dental floss / Bill Myers.
p. cm. — (The Incredible worlds of Wally McDoogle ; #5)
Summary: Bumbling but brilliant Wally McDoogle learns that honesty is the best policy after a practical joke snowballs into near disaster involving terrorists, tourists, television news, and the President.
ISBN 978-0-8499-3537-4 (trade paper)
[1. Honesty—Fiction. 2. Christian life—Fiction. 3. Humorous stories.] I. Title. II. Series: Myers, Bill, 1953– .
Incredible worlds of Wally McDoogle ; #5.
PZ7.M9822My 1994
[Fic]—dc20

93-47257
CIP
AC

Printed in the United States of America

20 21 22 23 24 LSC 5 4 3 2 1

For Paul Anderson—
A man of truth and integrity.

Whoever is careful about what he says protects his life. But anyone who speaks without thinking will be ruined.

—Proverbs 13:3

Contents

Chapter 1

Just for Starters

If you think this book is about dinosaurs, forget it. Put it back on the shelf. Send it back to the bookstore. Tell Mom or Grandma or whoever gave it to you, "Thanks, but no thanks!"

Believe me, after this, my latest adventure in the land of Me-and-My-Big-Mouth, the last thing in the world I want to do is tell any more lies.

The truth is . . .

—I've never known any real dinosaurs.
—I've never even seen a real dinosaur . . . although I am grateful to a certain *Tyrannosaurus Rex* for saving my life.

Confused?

Me too. But I'm Wally McDoogle, and that's normal for me. Let's see if I can help straighten things out for you.

It all started last Tuesday. We were on a class field trip at the Middletown Museum of Natural History. Our tour guide was rattling off a bunch of brain-numbing facts while our science teacher, Mr. Reptenson (better known as Reptile Man), kept acting like this information would save the world.

Of course everyone was bored out of their skulls. Not bored like having-to-sit-at-the-dinner-table-and-wait-until-everyone-else-is-finished-eating bored. No sir, we're talking out-of-your-mind,

I'd-rather-be-home-emptying-the-dishwasher-or-even-watching-*Sesame Street*-reruns kind of bored.

Everyone was bored, that is, except me and my best friend and fellow Dork-oid, Opera. We weren't bored because we'd found a powerful new secret weapon.

LYING

That's right. Forget about having to work; forget about having to study; forget about all that stuff. Just make it up.

Don't want to go to school?
How 'bout: "Mom, I've got the flu."

Want to impress that new girl?
How 'bout: "My dad is Mr. Incredible."

And let's not forget the ever-popular:
"I don't have my homework 'cause my pet aardvark ate it."

See how simple it is?

Simple, yes. Smart? Well, you tell me.

In the beginning, our lying spree had helped us talk the bus driver into letting us sit up front because we got "bus sick." Next, we convinced the new kid that we were outer-space visitors from the planet Ursodumb. And after that we almost convinced Reptile Man that his watch was an hour behind. (That was Opera's idea—he was hoping for an early lunch. He has a little thing about eating—actually a big thing. But he hates anything healthy—it's junk food or nothing. In fact, he's the only kid I know who gets convulsions over the smell of fresh fruit and vegetables. He's also the only kid I know who chews potato chip-flavored bubble gum.)

Anyway, things were going pretty well at the museum, except that the *Tyrannosaurus Rex* room was closed for repairs. Too bad. The giant dinosaur display was the main reason we had come. But I wasn't worried. With a few well-placed lies, I was sure I could get in to see it . . . no sweat.

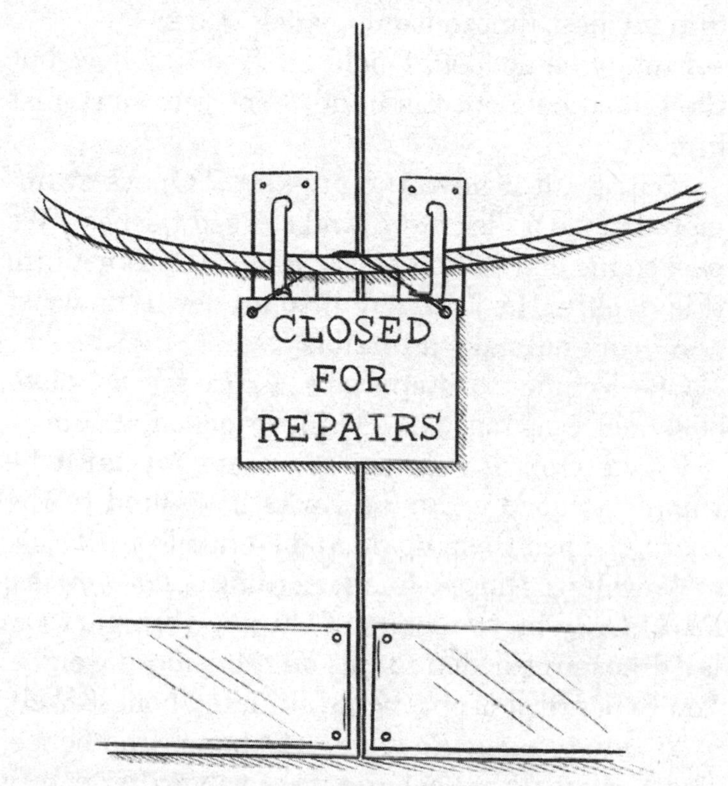

"Excuse me," I said to the guard sitting near the closed doors. I held out my lunch sack. "This is for my dad."

"Your dad?" the guard asked.

"Yeah, he's working inside there on the dinosaur display."

The guard gave me a careful look over.

I blinked at him, pushed up my glasses, and gave him my best innocent-puppy-dog stare.

Finally he nodded. Opera started to follow, but the guard held out his hand. "Not you, son—just him."

"But, I, uh, I have the napkins," Opera stammered as he pulled out a wad of used tissues. "We packed his dad a fresh peach, and if I don't get him this napkin, the juice will drip all down his wrist and arm and make a terrible . . ."

Opera came to a stop. It was a nice try, but obviously not working. The man just looked at him.

I gave Opera a shrug. It wasn't my fault he wasn't as good a liar as I was. I walked to the doors, pushed them open, and stepped inside.

Wow! It was huge—like something out of *Jurassic Park*! Only by the looks of things, this particular dinosaur needed to put on a bit more weight. You've heard of people being skin and bones? Well, ol' *Tyrannosaurus Rex* here was bones and bones. That's right, from her tail all the way to her pointy fangs, she was just your basic dinosaur skeleton. But even at that, I'd still hate to meet her in a dark, prehistoric alley.

There were five or six guys in overalls working on

her. Most were up on ladders, so no one really noticed when I sneaked up to the towering giant . . . Mistake Number One. (Well, actually Number Two, if you count the lying I did to get inside.)

Next, I reached out and touched the critter's right leg bone. (Mistake Number Three, if you're still keeping score.) But the touching wasn't the problem. It was the letting go. I couldn't. They had coated the whole thing in some sort of liquid plastic—a liquid plastic that hadn't dried yet. A liquid plastic that was great for protecting the skeleton, but bad for me—unless I wanted to be a permanent part of the display. In short, I was stuck big time.

I tried pulling my hand away. Nothing. I pulled harder. Still nothing. I set down my lunch sack and tugged with everything I had.

"Oooo . . . ahhh . . . eeee . . ."

At last, something gave. Unfortunately, it wasn't my hand. It was the leg bone. The entire thing popped out of its socket.

"Uh-oh!"

The skeleton started to creak. Everyone stopped working. They looked around until they spotted me. I tried to hide the bone behind my back—a little tricky since it was about five and a half feet long, and I'm about five and no half feet tall.

I flashed them my famous McDoogle-the-Idiot grin.

No one smiled back.

The skeleton continued to groan and creak. It was beginning to tilt.

"*She's coming down*!" someone cried.

That someone was right. Thanks to the little leg amputation I'd just performed, Ol' Rexy girl thought it was time to lie down—fast! Suddenly it started raining. But not water. It was raining dinosaur bones! That's right—teeth, vertebrae, arms, you name it. It was coming down like cats and dogs . . . well, actually, like tibias and fibulas (that's bone talk in case any of you want to be doctors).

The workers leaped off their ladders and ran for the doors screaming, "*Look out*! *Look out*!"

Wanting to participate in the fun and games, I joined in with a little running and screaming of my own.

"AUGH!"

Actually a lot of screaming.

"AUGHHHHHHHHHHHHHHHHHH!"

Suddenly Rexy gave me a hand—literally. Her right paw crashed down on my shoulder like a huge prehistoric pat on the back and sent me sprawling to the ground.

"OOAAAFFFF!"

It was then when I noticed my lunch sack near the door. Funny. It was a dozen yards from where I set it down. I dragged myself toward it. I didn't do this because I was hungry; I did it because I was planning ahead. I figured I'd need a decent meal before dying. (I just hoped that my lunch had been packed by Mom and not by my little sister.)

At last, I reached my sack. I scooped it up, jumped to my feet, and raced for the door just as . . .

K-BOOM!

I looked over my shoulder. Ol' Rexy had finished "going to pieces." Instead of a noble dinosaur, she looked like a giant pile of Pick-Up Sticks. I didn't know it then, but within thirty-two hours this giant boneyard would be reassembled and would save my life.

And that's no lie.

* * * * *

Maybe it was the lecture by the head museum guy or his call to my parents. Or maybe it was Mom's promise that when I got home she'd ground me for the rest of my life (and longer if they'd let her continue it in heaven). The point is, as we rode home on the bus, I began to wonder if this lying business was such a good idea after all. Oh sure, I know we're taught in Sunday school not to do it, but I guess there are some things a guy's got to find out on his own.

CRUNCH! MUSH-MUSH-MUSH! CRUNCH! MUSH-MUSH-MUSH.

I threw a look over at Opera. He was starting in on his lunch—three bags of extra-crispy, salt-saturated, deep-fried fat . . . with a little bit of potato thrown in the middle so they could call them *potato* chips. That's what all the *crunch*ing was about. The *mush-mush-mush*ing was the sound made by the chips after he dipped them into his ketchup.

"That's gross," I groaned.

"I know," he yelled over his headphones as he stuffed another handful of the chips into his mouth. "But I couldn't find my special mixture of maple syrup and mustard."

I shuddered and reached for my own lunch sack. It was a little worn from all the kicking around in the dinosaur room, and for some reason it seemed a little bigger than I remembered. When I reached inside I found an even greater surprise.

"What in the world?" I said as I pulled out a giant jar of reddish-pink gunk. It was thick and gooey and so bright it might have glowed in the dark.

"Looks like your sister's been busy in the kitchen again," Opera shouted over his music.

"I don't think so," I answered as I carefully turned the jar over in my hands. I'd never seen anything like it. I looked back in the bag. "I think I've got the wrong sack here. This isn't my lunch."

"I'll sell you mine." Wall Street turned around in the seat in front of us. As my other best friend, Wall Street was determined to make her first million by the time she was fourteen. And by the way she was always ripping me off, I knew she'd owe much of her success to me.

"You want to sell me your lunch?" I asked. "How much?"

"Normally . . ." she scrunched up her eyebrows to think. "Normally $3.95, but since we're best friends, I'll let you have it for 5 bucks even."

"Sold," I said. (I told you she was good.)

"What do you think that stuff is?" Wall Street asked as she handed over her lunch and took my money.

"Got me," I said. "Just your basic nuclear toxic waste."

"You're kidding!" she exclaimed.

For a business tycoon, Wall Street was still pretty gullible. I threw a look over at Opera. If she believed that big of a whopper, we could really have fun with her. Fortunately, Opera and I had both had enough lying for now.

Unfortunately, *for now* isn't exactly the same as *forever.*

Chapter 2

News at Eleven

Opera spent the night at my place—not because Mom and Dad were passing out rewards for my "Destroy the Dinosaur" routine, but because his folks were out of town at a convention. We were up in my room so bored that we were actually watching the news. Cindy Cho was rambling on about some nuclear power plant being broken into. Nobody knew if anything was missing or who was responsible, but some folks were afraid it might be terrorists.

For the last half hour Opera had been trying to open the container of reddish-pink gunk, but no luck. "What did you tell Wall Street this stuff was?" he asked.

"I don't remember . . . nuclear something. Why?"

He glanced at Cindy on the TV and then broke into a devious smile. Without a word, he reached for the his cell and punched in a number.

"What are you doing?" I asked Opera.

He held out his hand for me to be quiet. There was no missing the gleam in his eye. Finally he spoke into the phone. "Hello, Wall Street? Yeah, it's me. Listen, the weirdest thing just happened. Remember that pink stuff Wally found? Well, some terrorist guys just called and said we better hand it over or there would be big trouble."

I had to smile. Opera's *tall tales* were getting taller.

"Why do they want it?" he said, repeating her question and looking to me for help. "Well, uh, because, uh . . ." The guy was a definite amateur. He was already in trouble.

I bailed him out by whispering, "Because it's the makings of a nuclear bomb?" (Hey, if you're going to tell a whopper, go for the big ones.)

Opera grinned and spoke into the phone, "Because they're using it to make a bomb to blow something up. What?" Again he looked to me for help. "Well, I don't know what they wanted to blow up . . . uh . . . maybe . . . er . . ."

"The museum," I whispered. "Tell her it was supposed to be the museum."

"Yeah, it was supposed to be the museum," he gratefully repeated.

Now, like I said, I had been wondering about all this lying stuff. But Opera definitely needed some help. And since Pastor Swenson always says, "Use your God-given gifts to help others," I did just that. I gave Opera everything I had.

I raced to the door and began banging on it. "*Open up*!" I shouted in my best bad-guy voice. "*We know you're in there*! *Open up*!"

Opera started to giggle. "Oh no," he managed to choke out, "they're at our door!"

I banged some more and shouted, *"If you don't open up, we're going to blow you to kingdom come!"*

"Oh no!" Opera motioned for me to keep knocking and shouting. "What do we do? What do we do?!"

I banged and shouted even louder.

"Oh no!" Opera repeated. *"Oh, no . . . don't—get away . . . get away . . . get—"* And then he hung up. Just like that. Right in the middle of his sentence. I tell you, for an amateur, he was learning quickly.

We exploded into laughter. "I can just see the look on her face," I cried, trying to catch my breath.

"You think we really had her fooled?" Opera gasped.

"You know Wall Street," I said. "She'll believe anything. And the way you hung up—perfect."

"Your sound effects were great!"

Suddenly the phone rang.

"That's her!" Opera giggled. "I know it's her."

The phone rang again. I motioned for him to be quiet, then I accepted the call. But I didn't say a word.

Wall Street was on the other end. "Opera . . . is that you?" She really sounded worried. "Opera . . . Wally . . . are you guys okay?"

Now I basically had two choices. I could bust

a gut laughing and let her know it was just a joke . . . or I could keep playing along. I knew what I *should* do. But I also knew I had company and was bored out of my mind. Besides, it wasn't my fault—Opera was the one who started the lie.

"Guys . . . ?" Wall Street said. "Are you okay?"

I covered the mouthpiece with part of my shirt and spoke in my best accent: "I am so sorry, but they are all . . ." I swallowed back a giggle. "They are all tied up at the moment. Who is this?"

There was a long silence.

I repeated, "May I have your name and address?"

Suddenly there was a loud click. Wall Street had hung up.

Opera and I burst out laughing again. It was great. Too good to be true.

Unfortunately, it would soon become too true to be good.

* * * * *

An hour later Opera was lost in another *The Big Bang Theory* rerun. I had seen it about a hundred times, and Opera was getting more than a little mad at me for saying every line before they said it. So I reached over and grabbed ol' Betsy, my laptop. It was definitely time to work on another one of my world-famous fantasies.

BUBBLE—BUBBLE—BUBBLE...

BUBBLE—BUBBLE—BUBBLE...

It is Hydro Dude McDoogle's telephone hotline—the one connected to Washington DC's Plight House where

President Bill Franklin lives. As a world-renowned superhero and part-time Amway distributor, the liquid Hydro Dude is always receiving such calls. Usually it's when the Plight House runs out of laundry soap or industrial strength cleanser. But not this time.

"Bubbllo," our superhero answers.

"Hydro Dude!" It is the president himself. "We have an emergency!"

"Running out of dishwashing liquid?" Hydro Dude asks in concern.

"Worse than that. Your archenemy, the dreaded Dr. Yes, is on the rampage again."

"No!" our hero cries.

"No," the president corrects.

"I thought you just said it was Yes."

"Yes, it is Yes."

"But, Mr. President, you just said it was, 'No.'"

"I said, 'No, it's not No...'"

"But yes, it's Yes?"

"Yes...it's Dr. Yes."

Hydro Dude scratches his head. Talking to politicians can get kinda confusing. "Mr. President, could we start again?"

"We desperately need your help! Dr.

Yes is releasing a deadly toxin into the air. It is vaporizing the letter *B*."

"You mean the letter *B* is disappearing?"

"Yes!"

"No!" our hero cries in disbelief.

"No, it's 'Yes!'" the president corrects.

"Mr. President, could we not get into that again? Are you telling me that Dr. Yes is erasing the letter *B* from the alphabet?"

"Yes!" the president cries.

"Like from books and newspapers and—"

"But not just the letter! His formula is vaporizing anything that starts with the letter *B*!"

Hydro Dude looks around his bedroom. The president is right. All the Books on his shelves are starting to grow faint and disappear. He glances over to the Basketball near his door. It is also disappearing. Even the light Bulb in his lamp is going.

"You must hurry, Hydro Dude..."

"Hello, Mr. President? You'll have to speak up. I can barely hear you."

"I'm fading too..." The voice on the other end is barely above a whisper.

"But that's impossible. You're the president! There's no *B* in president!"

"But my first name is Bill.... Hurry...."

Suddenly they are disconnected.

"Mr. President! Mr. President!"

Hydro Dude slams down the phone. It's going to be a tough job, but he knows he has to do what he has to do, so he decides he better do it...(or something like that).

No one knows how Hydro Dude first became liquid. Some say it was his mom making him drink too many fluids when he had a fever. Others say it was having to take too many baths. Then there's the ever-popular theory that it happened when he had to sit in the backseat of the car too long. He kept complaining that the sun was too hot and that he was melting, but nobody paid him any attention...until he finally did just that...melted. He completely melted into a puddle of little dude goo.

Whatever the reason, Hydro Dude must once again use his superpowers for good. He quickly (and quite literally) pours himself into his clothes and sloshes toward the door.

"You're not going outside without an umbrella!" his mom calls from the kitchen.

"Oh, Mom..."

"Don't 'Oh, Mom' me," she says, drying her hands and heading toward him. You may be Mr. Fancy Schmanzy Superhero to the rest of the universe, but you're still my little squirt."

"Oh, Mom..."

She gives him a pinch on the cheek, which causes part of him to spurt between her fingers and land on the floor. (He hates it when she does that.)

She grabs a dry cloth, quickly wipes up the floor, and wrings out the liquid over his head. "It's hotter than blazes out there today."

"Yes, Mom."

"And if you don't stay under an umbrella, you know that sun will completely evaporate you!"

"Yes, Mom."

"And furthermore..."

Is it his imagination, or is her voice growing fainter too? He looks at her. Great Scott! She's also fading! And then he remembers that her name really isn't Mom, but...Bertha!

He must find Dr. Yes. If he doesn't, who will bundle him up in the winter so he doesn't turn into an ice sculpture? Who will make up his *water*bed every morning? And most importantly, who will sew up the rips in his clothes so he doesn't leak out all over the place?

Quickly, our hero throws open the door and races outside in search of the devastatingly dastardly Dr. Yes.

Then, suddenly—

"Hey, Wally . . ."

I glanced up from ol' Betsy. Opera was standing at the side of my window, squinting through the curtains.

"What's up?" I hated being interrupted from one of my stories, but Opera sounded a little nervous.

"Do any of your neighbors like to, you know, run around with ropes and dress all in black with ski masks and carry fully automatic assault rifles?"

I smirked. "Not on Tuesday nights. We usually save that for Thursdays when—"

"I'm not kidding, Wally." His voice definitely sounded a little shaky. "Take a look."

I hopped off the bed and poked my head out the window. "I don't see any—"

"Over there," he pointed to a nearby bush.

I peered into the darkness. At first all I saw was a bush. Now normally that wouldn't be too unusual, except there had never been a bush in that part of the yard before . . . and even if there had been, it wouldn't be walking toward the house . . . or carrying a walkie-talkie and machine gun!

"And there." Opera pointed to a nearby tree. Nothing too unusual—just the old mulberry tree we used to climb . . . except for the giant rifle with a scope sticking out from behind it . . . a giant rifle with a scope pointing directly at me!

I ducked away from the window and cried, "What's going on?"

"Got me." Opera shrugged. "Halloween's in six months. It's a little early for trick-or-treaters."

My heart started to pound. For a moment I thought I might be in one of my own superhero stories, but ol' Betsy was on the bed, and I was way over by the window. I was a great typist but not that great.

It was time to act bravely. It was time for incredible boldness and outstanding courage. It was time to cry out to Mommy and Daddy for help. But before I could open my mouth, the phone rang.

RING.

Opera and I looked at each other. "Go ahead," Opera whispered. "Answer it."

RING.

"You're closer," I whispered back.

"But it's your phone," he argued.

RING.

"What's that got to do with it?"

"If it's the wrong number," he explained, "and they ask what number they're calling, you'll be able to tell them 'cause it's yours and you know it better than I do."

I gave him a look. The only thing worse than his tall-tale telling was his excuse making.

RING.

With a heavy sigh I dropped to my knees (out of sight from the dancing bush and the gun-slinging tree) and pulled out my phone. I picked it up and answered. "Hello?"

There was a brief crackle. Then a harsh, gritty voice said, "Ve have zee place surrounded. Throw down zee nuclear material and no von vill get hurt."

"W-what?" I shot Opera a terrified look. He scampered over to me and pressed his ear near mine to listen. The voice repeated itself evenly and calmly—the accent was strong. "Ve have zee place surrounded and ve vant zee nuclear fuel you stole—vee vant it now."

"Uh . . . yeah . . . sure . . ." I stammered. "Uh, one nuclear fuel coming right up." I quickly disconnected.

"Nuclear fuel?" Opera echoed. "What nuclear fuel? Who are those guys?!"

I shook my head. He had raised a couple of good questions. Unfortunately, I didn't have any good answers . . . until my eye landed on the reddish-pink gunk still in the jar lying on my bed.

Could it be . . . ?

Opera followed my gaze to the jar. His eyes widened. "No way," he whispered.

I tried to swallow, but at the moment there wasn't much in my mouth to swallow.

"You think . . . you think it really is nuclear fuel?" Opera asked.

"I don't know," I croaked. "But you heard the news on TV. Somebody broke into a nuclear plant and . . . "

"And you . . . you accidentally got *their* sack instead . . ." Opera shook his head. "Wait a minute—that's the story we told Wall Street."

"You heard them," I said. "Maybe it wasn't a story after all."

We both stared at the jar. It sure looked weird. To be honest, neither of us had ever seen anything quite like it.

"Could it be?" Opera asked.

I shook my head, even more clueless than normal.

Opera's mind continued to spin. "And if that's really nuclear fuel . . . then those are the guys who stole it and want it back . . . and that makes them . . ." his voice dropped off.

I slowly nodded and finished his sentence, "The terrorists."

Chapter 3

On the Lam

Opera dropped to his knees out of sight from the window and started crawling and squirming on his belly toward the bed. It was not a pretty sight. He obviously hadn't had much experience crawling and squirming because with every two feet he crawled forward, he managed to squirm one foot backward.

"What are you doing?" I asked.

He made it to the bed and grabbed the jar of reddish-pink gunk. "They want this stuff," he said. "Let's give it to them." He dropped back to his stomach and repeated the same pathetic crawling routine back toward the window.

"No way!" I hopped to the floor and grabbed the jar from him. "Those are terrorists out there!"

"Yeah, I noticed." He grabbed the jar back from me.

"So, if we give this to them, they'll use it to blow something up." I grabbed the jar back from him.

"If we *don't* give it to them, they'll blow *us* up." He grabbed the jar back from me.

"Opera!" I cried.

"Wally!" he shouted.

"Opera!" I repeated.

"Wally!" he re-repeated.

So much for meaningful conversation. We were getting nowhere fast. Suddenly I had a brainstorm—well, actually, more like a "brain drizzle." But at least it was something.

I reached for the phone.

"What are you doing?" Opera demanded.

"I'm calling the police," I said. "They'll know what to—"

Suddenly the accented voice spoke from the other end. "You have five minutes to make zee decision, or ve're coming in after you." They were still on the line. I ended the call.

"Wrong number?" Opera asked hopefully.

I shook my head. "Okay, listen," I said, "we can't give them the gunk or they'll blow something up. We can't stay herc or they'll blow us up."

"So what do we do?"

"I guess we'll have to make a run for it."

"*Run*?" Opera repeated. It obviously wasn't one of his favorite words. Eat? Yes. Watch TV? Absolutely. Listen to classical music on his tape player? Oh yeah. But, running or doing anything physical . . . ?

"Oh no," he said.

"There's no other way," I insisted.

Opera took a deep breath and gave me one of his okay-but-if-we-die-you're-going-to-live-to-regret-it looks. In a flash, he rose to his feet, flung the covers off my bed, and started tying my sheets together.

"What are you doing?" I asked.

"I saw it on TV—if you're in a second-story room, you tie the sheets together, fasten them to the bed, and climb out the window."

I nodded. "We could do that, but wouldn't taking the stairs be easier?"

He dropped the sheets. "Good point."

I grabbed the reddish-pink gunk. We dropped to our knees and quickly crawled toward the door.

Well, I quickly crawled. Opera was still having some difficulty in that department.

When we finally reached the hall, we stood and headed for the stairs. Of course the rest of the family was asleep—Mom, Dad, my older twin brothers, Burt and Brock, and my little sister, Carrie. I thought about waking Mom and telling her, but if she was upset about my clumsiness with the dinosaur, she'd really fret if she thought I was holding a jar that could blow up half the United States.

We started down the stairs. So far, so good. Well, except for the part where I stepped on my sister's cat, Collision.

I could give you the details, but let's just say Collision didn't get her name by accident. Basically, she was always at the wrong place, doing the wrong thing, at the wrong time. Like sleeping in the dryer whenever Mom thought it was time to tumble dry the clothes. Or gnawing on the extension cord to our Christmas-tree lights (the tree wasn't the only thing that "lit up" that year). Or snuggling up to Dad's fan belt on those nice cold mornings just before he got into his car and drove off to work.

Yes sir, ol' Collision definitely had had her moments . . . which explained why she was always a little lacking in the fur department.

Anyway . . .

REEEEOOOOWWWW! (That was Collision, screaming.)

TUMBLE, TUMBLE. "Ouch! Ouch!" *TUMBLE, BOUNCE, ROLL* . . . (That was me, falling down the stairs.)

At last I hit bottom.

BANG! GROAN!

A moment later, Opera was at my side, smothering me with all sorts of concern and sympathy. "Don't be a jerk, McDoogle. Stop clowning around!"

He helped me up, but I stepped on Collision again.

REEEEOOOOWWWW!

BANG! GROAN! (We were in a hurry, so I decided to leave out the *TUMBLE, TUMBLE,* "Ouch! Ouch!" *TUMBLE, BOUNCE, ROLL* part.)

Once I was back to my feet, Opera reached for the front door—the very same front door that the terrorists had been sneaking up to.

I grabbed Opera's arm and suggested, "Maybe the back basement window would be less obvious."

He saw my point.

We headed for the basement. Luckily, Collision had not made it to those stairs yet. She probably wanted to stay some place safer, such as inside the microwave oven.

When we reached the bottom of the stairs, I pointed toward the back window. "Over there."

In no time flat, we climbed on the laundry table, peeked out the window, and started crawling through it. It was a little difficult for Opera (like I said, crawling wasn't his best skill), but with lots of grunting and more than the daily minimum requirement of groaning, we finally made it out. We staggered to our feet and looked around. Fortunately,

there were no wandering bushes or armed trees in sight.

We quickly ran toward the back gate. Unfortunately, it wasn't quickly enough.

"There they are!" a voice shouted.

We were hit by a glaring light. But it wasn't a searchlight. Oh no, we couldn't be that lucky. This was a TV camera light . . . complete with a cameraman and reporter!

"Go for a close-up!" a woman's voice shouted. "Go for a close-up!" It was Cindy Cho, news reporter.

Now Opera and I had two choices: Stick around and be dead TV stars . . . or run like the wind and be living chickens. It was a tough choice, but let's just say Colonel Sanders would have been proud. We raced through the back gate and into the alley.

Suddenly there was a squeal of tires. I looked over my shoulder and saw a gray van bearing down on us. But it wasn't a news van. And its lights were off like it didn't want to attract attention.

"In here!" I shouted, as we raced into another backyard.

GROWL, BARK, BARK, SNARL!

"Uh, maybe not."

We changed directions and cut through the next yard, running for all we were worth.

* * * * *

An hour and a half later we arrived at Wall Street's house. (It would have been ten minutes later, but Opera is an even worse runner than he is a crawler.) We threw pebbles against Wall Street's window until she finally looked out. When she saw us, she opened the front door.

"Come on in," she whispered so she wouldn't wake up her mom. "You guys are really famous."

"What are you talking about?" Opera wheezed as we staggered inside.

"Take a look." She pointed to the TV.

It was newswoman Cindy Cho again. She stood in front of a house that looked a lot like mine and she was interviewing people who looked a lot like Mom and Dad. The reason was fairly simple: It *was* my house, and it *was* Mom and Dad!

"No," Dad was saying, "it's some sort of mix-up. I just can't believe it's him . . ."

"Who's he talking about?" I asked.

"You," Wall Street answered.

"What?"

"Shhh." She motioned for me to be quiet so she could hear.

Now Mom was on the screen, dabbing her eyes and saying, "He always seemed like such a normal child."

"But Mom . . ." It was my little sister, Carrie, trying to get in on the act. "Don't you remember that smashed burrito incident last summer or how he destroyed the movie studio's alien monster or how he almost died with that broken bungee cord or how he was nearly eaten by that crocodile in South America?"

"Oh . . ." Mom looked less sure.

"And don't forget what he did to the dinosaur this afternoon."

"Yes," Mom hesitated. "I, uh, I see your point."

I turned to Wall Street. "What's going on?"

She pointed to the jar of reddish-pink gunk I still had in my hand. "Is that what you're going to blow up the museum with?" she asked.

"What?" I cried with wide eyes. "Wall Street, what's going on?"

"After you called me and said you had nuclear stuff and that terrorists were trying to get it from you—"

"That was just a joke," Opera interrupted.

"A *joke*?" she repeated, her voice quivering.

I nodded. "Yeah, we were just fooling."

"Oh . . . after you hung up, I was so worried that I called the police."

"The police?" Opera and I cried in two-part harmony.

"Well . . . yeah. I honestly thought you guys were in trouble."

I gave Opera a look.

Wall Street continued, "So they sent out a SWAT team to save you from the terrorists."

"But there weren't any terrorists," I repeated. "Not at first. That was all made up."

"Look." She pointed toward the TV. "There's the leader of the SWAT team now."

A man dressed in black with a couple of tree branches sticking out of his stocking hat was being interviewed. His voice sounded strangely familiar. "And zen vee called zem up on zee phone and gave zem five minutes to surrender and—"

"Oh no," I groaned, turning to Opera. "That was the man on the telephone. He wasn't a terrorist. He was a SWAT guy. Oh no," I groaned again.

Opera looked like he wanted to do some groaning of his own, but it's hard to groan when your jaw is hanging to the floor.

"Look at this." Wall Street motioned back to the TV.

Cindy Cho was playing a video in slow motion. But not just any video. This particular video happened to be the one they made of me and Opera running toward the back gate. "And here," Cindy Cho said, "we can clearly see the two terrorists escaping. Because of the shadows it's impossible to make out this chubby lad, but we have definite confirmation that the other one is Mr. Wallace McDoogle."

"They think I'm a terrorist?" I cried.

"Shhh . . ." Opera and Wall Street both motioned for me to be quiet.

Cindy Cho continued, "Now, if we can freeze the video right here . . ." The video stopped. "There . . . see," she said, "look under his arm—that canister . . . it's apparently the stolen nuclear material with which he plans to build his bomb."

"Bomb?" I cried. "Who said anything about a bomb?"

Wall Street answered, "When you called, you said the terrorists were going to build a bomb and—"

"But that was all made up," I protested.

"How'd I know?"

The pieces were coming together in a rough sort of way. I was getting the world's worst headache. "And because they have me on video, running away with this jar," I said slowly, "they think I'm the terrorist?"

"Bingo," Wall Street grinned.

"Look," Opera pointed at the TV, "there's your brother Brock."

I leaned forward to listen. Good ol' Brock. Brock knew I wouldn't do anything like that. Brock would straighten things out. That's what loving, big brothers were for, right?

"I always knew he had a screw loose," Brock said, shaking his head. "But for him to pull a stunt like this . . ."

"What?" I shouted at the TV.

"Shhh," Wall Street and Opera both whispered.

Brock continued, "I guess it's like they always say, it's the quiet ones you got to watch out for."

So much for loving brothers. I closed my eyes. If I thought my head hurt before, it was nothing compared to the jackhammers going on inside it now. On the McDoogle Weirdness Scale of one to ten, this was definitely somewhere in the hundreds.

Unfortunately, that number would continue to climb.

Chapter 4

The Plot Sickens

I turned to Opera and asked, "What do we do?"

He shrugged and turned to Wall Street. "Got any chips?" (Good ol' Opera. Some people have their teddy bears and security blankets. Opera's got his junk food.)

"You should probably call the police," Wall Street offered.

"But they think I'm the terrorist!" I argued. "I'm the one they talked to on the phone. I'm the one on the video. I'm the one with this nuclear gunk."

We all paused to look at the canister of reddish-pink goo in my hand. Who could have believed that one little jar could cause all this trouble? Then again, maybe it wasn't one little jar that had caused the trouble; maybe it was one little lie.

"I still think you should call," Wall Street said, nodding toward the phone on the table.

I took a deep breath and slowly let it out. Maybe

she was right. Maybe the police would understand. Maybe I could clear all this up. Maybe they'd only throw me in jail for thirty or forty years. I reached for my phone, but before I could call, it rang.

We looked at one another in surprise.

Wall Street reached for it and answered. "Hello?"

Opera and I exchanged glances. Now what?

Wall Street covered the mouthpiece, "It's Cindy Cho," she whispered. "She found out I'm your friend and wants to know if I've heard from you."

"Go ahead." I nodded. "If we're telling the police, we might as well tell everybody."

Wall Street spoke into the phone. "Yes, I have. As a matter of fact, he's right here. Yes, he's standing right across from me and . . . Hello? Hello?" Wall Street lowered the phone. "She hung up."

"She's on her way," I said.

"Looks like you're going to be a TV star after all." Opera grinned.

Before I could answer, there was a loud knocking at the door.

We all froze. It couldn't be Cindy Cho. Not that soon. I crept to the window and peeked through

the drapes. "It's the gray van," I said. "Probably the police. They must have followed us."

They knocked again. Louder.

"Go ahead," I said to Wall Street, "before they bruise their knuckles. Open it up and let's face the music."

She walked over to the door and unlocked it. Suddenly it was thrown open by two people wearing ski masks. They stumbled in, tripped over each other, and managed to wind up in a big knot of arms and legs on the floor.

"Get off me, you big lug!" the smaller one cried. It sounded like a woman.

"It's these ski masks," the big lug protested. "I can't see a thing."

At last they scrambled to their feet.

"All right, McDoogle," the woman shouted from underneath her ski mask. She pointed a shotgun directly at Wall Street. "Hand it over."

I cleared my throat behind her. "Uh, officer, I'm Wally McDoogle."

The woman spun around, hitting her partner in the stomach with the gun barrel.

"OAAF," the big lug cried. "That hurt!"

"I didn't see you," the woman snapped.

"It's these ski masks," Big Lug whined.

"Will you please be quiet!"

"Wait a minute," I interrupted. "Are you guys really police?"

The woman swiveled back and forth trying to find me.

"Uh, over here." I waved.

Finally she spotted me and readjusted her mask. "Who said we were police? We're terrorists."

"Terrorists?" I gasped.

"Yes, we're part of a new terrorist organization."

"What are you called?"

She cleared her voice and proudly proclaimed, "We are the local chapter of an organization called Save the Snails."

"Save the Snails?"

"That's right," Big Lug said and nodded.

We were dumbfounded.

Big Lug continued, "Have you any idea how much torture we humans inflict on poor, innocent snails?"

"Well, I, uh, I never really stopped to—"

"We step on them, we poison them . . ." There was no missing the emotion growing in his voice. "We grind them into the dirt, and . . . " He gave a little shudder and almost started to sob, "and . . . some people . . . some people even eat them!"

We all watched as Big Lug finally broke down right there in front of us. Wall Street grabbed a box of tissues and handed it to him. He blew his nose (not an easy thing to do inside a ski mask) and tried to regain control.

After a moment, Opera said, "But I've never even heard of you guys before."

"That's why we're here," the woman answered. "We heard on the police radio that you stole some nuclear fuel, and we've come to get it to make our own bomb!"

"But I never stole—"

"Yeah," Big Lug interrupted as he handed the box of tissues back to Wall Street. "We're going to build our own bomb and blow something up real good so everyone will pay attention to our cause and—"

"Honey?" It was Wall Street's mom calling from the upstairs bedroom. I guess all the loud voices finally woke her up.

Wall Street threw a panicked look at all of us. The terrorists waved their guns, motioning that they weren't in the mood for company.

"Honey?" her mother repeated. "Are you still up?"

Wall Street swallowed hard and answered, "Yes, Momma, I'm still up."

"Well, turn down that silly TV show, will you? It's making too much racket."

"Okay, Momma."

Apparently she thought all of our voices were just a silly show. Maybe she had a point. Anyway, we all let out a sigh of relief. But not for long.

Suddenly there was the sound of squealing brakes. I looked out the window. Another van. On its side were the words WART-TV. Immediately Cindy Cho and her cameraman piled out.

"It's the newspeople," I said.

"That means the cops are on the way!" the woman cried to her partner. "Let's run for it!" She spun around and crashed into the big guy. Once again they began their Three Stooges routine of standing and falling.

Now was my chance. No way would I let these bungling bad guys have this nuclear fuel (or whatever it was). I tucked the canister under my arm and made a break for the door. As I threw it open I was met by a glaring TV light and Cindy Cho's microphone.

"Mr. McDoogle—would you care to tell us why you want to blow up the Museum of Natural History?"

I opened my mouth, ready to spill the beans, ready to set everything straight, when Big Lug suddenly grabbed me from behind. "'Cause he's with us!" he shouted through his mask as he dragged me to his van. His partner was close behind.

Cindy Cho followed. "But who are you—what are your intentions?"

Big Lug opened the van's back door and sort of half-helped, half-threw me into the back.

WHOAAA!

"Your names," Cindy Cho cried. "What are your names? What is your purpose?"

"Our purpose is simple," the woman cried as

they hopped in the front and Big Lug cranked the engine. "We are here to . . . save the snails!"

With that we peeled out . . . well, sort of. First we managed to bounce up on the curb, wipe out a couple of prized begonias, then snap off the top of a nearby fire hydrant.

"You fool!" the woman screamed as water gushed high into the air and rained down on the windshield. "Get us out of here!"

"You don't have to yell," Big Lug whined as he turned on the wipers. "I've got feelings, you know. Just because I'm a man doesn't mean I'm out of touch with my—"

The woman's voice quivered as she tried to hold back her rage. "Will you *please* get us out of here?"

"There," he said and grinned, "you see how much nicer that sounds?"

He stomped on the accelerator, and we spun out. We hit the street hard and fishtailed down the road—all the time under the watchful eye of Cindy Cho's camera.

I'm not sure what demolition derby Big Lug got his driver's license from. But after four or five minutes of being a human pinball in the back of the van, I thought it might be time to make my escape. I edged toward the back door and reached for the lever.

It was now or never.

I threw open the door and WHOAAAA! The

asphalt zipped by at a zillion miles an hour! Maybe "never" of "now or never" wasn't such a bad idea after all.

The woman spun around and saw me. "He's going to jump!"

Before I could mention that I really wasn't interested in becoming the latest road kill and that I was allergic to dying, Big Lug slammed on the brakes. This sent me tumbling to the front of the van. Before I could stick around and chat, he swung the van into a hard 180-degree turn, which sent me bouncing backward along the floor of the van until suddenly there was no floor to be bouncing on. Now there was just that wonderful, boy-that-sure-smarts-when-you-hit-it asphalt.

I continued bouncing and tumbling . . . "Ouch! Ouch! Eech!" . . . until I hit some friendly bushes. *SCRATCH, SCRAPE, RIP* . . . and then a not-so-friendly tree.

K-BAMB!!

That, of course, was my head making contact with the tree. But for some reason I didn't feel any pain. I wasn't certain, but the best I figured, it probably had something to do with being knocked totally unconscious.

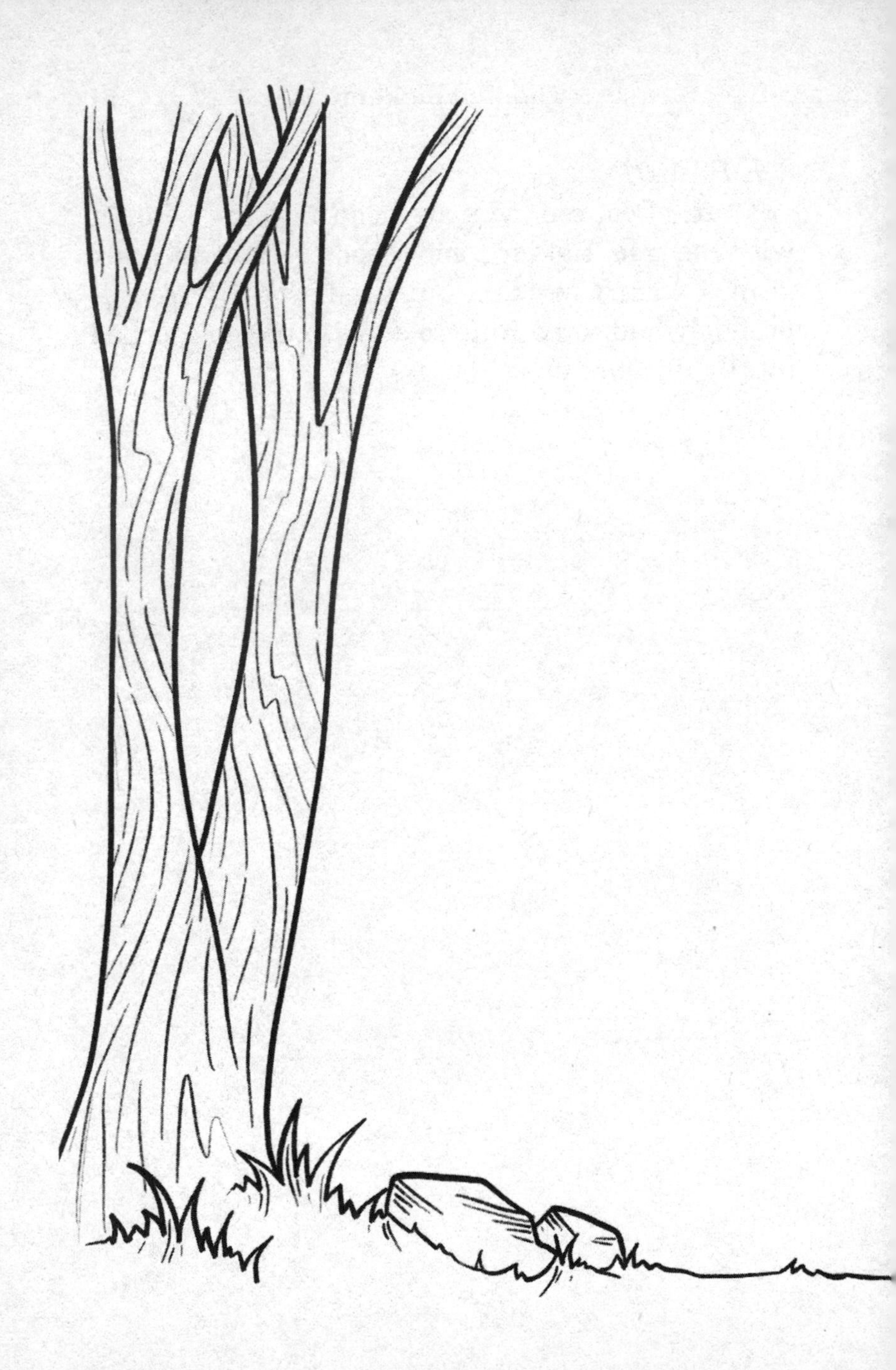

Chapter 5

So Much for Luck

I'm not sure how long it was before I woke up, but it definitely wasn't long enough. I don't want to complain, but my head pounded harder than a bass speaker in a rap song.

And my clothes? They were worse for wear, big time. Come to think about it, so was my body. But that was nothing compared to another minor problem.

My glasses. They were pretty much a complete disaster.

I slowly rose to my feet. The pounding in my head grew worse. I paused, patiently waiting to die. No luck. In fact, I couldn't even seem to pass out again. It just wasn't my day or, by the looks of things, my night.

I glanced around. Not that it did much good with my busted-up glasses. The best I could make out was that I was in some sort of park with trees.

Next I heard a *WHOOSH* and *SWHOOSH*. Definitely the sound of cars. They were about thirty feet away. Park . . . trees . . . busy street. My quick McDoogle mind went into action. I calculated everything around me, including the distance we had traveled in the van since we left Wall Street's place. A moment later I had the answer!

I was lost. Completely.

Then I heard the voices. "Over here," a man cried in the darkness. "Over here."

"Don't be an idiot," a female voice shouted. "He couldn't have rolled that far."

"Please, don't call me an idiot," the first voice whined. "You know how damaging that is to my low self-esteem."

There was no mistaking the owners of those voices. And there was no mistaking who they were looking for.

It was definitely time to get out of there. Now if I could only find my glasses. They had to be around there somewhere. I took half a step forward and—

CRUNCH!

Unfortunately that was half a step too far. I had smacked into a tree, and my glasses fell off. I dropped to the ground, fumbled to pick them up, and finally slipped them on.

Ahhh, much better. Well, except that both lenses were even more shattered. Now they looked like little spiderwebs. Little spiderwebs that, when you looked through, forced you to see seventeen images of the same thing. Still, seventeen images of the same thing was better than no images of anything.

At least I could see where I was. I stood in a park. The giant park with the Community Center across from our school.

The voices moved closer. "Over here! I'm certain he's over here!"

I had to get out of there fast. I turned and ran. There was a tree directly in front of me. Unfortunately, with my new designer glasses, it looked like seventeen trees. I wasn't sure which one to sidestep, but the odds were definitely in my favor. Sixteen of those images were wrong. There was only one real tree to miss so I ran forward, trusting in my good luck.

K-THUD!

So much for good luck.

As I fell backward, I landed on my old pal, the canister of reddish-pink gunk. Boy, oh boy, I'm sure glad I didn't forget that. Who knows how my life might have returned to normal if I'd left that behind. But now that I'd found it, I knew I had to take it.

"What was that?" Big Lug asked.

"I didn't hear anything," the woman snapped.

"It sounded like somebody hit a tree and fell."

"Don't be an idiot—nobody's that stupid."

I thought of speaking up and mentioning that I qualified for being that stupid, but since I was still kind of fond of living, I grabbed the canister, stood, and ran like the wind. Well, with my pounding head and aching body, I ran more like a gentle breeze. Actually, more like a slight draft.

A few minutes later, Olympic Heights Middle School came into view. I raced across the road and hesitated, trying to figure out which one of the seventeen entrances to the playground was real. After sixteen tries, I finally found it.

At the back of the playground there were seventeen baseball fields. Again, with my luck, I only made sixteen mistakes until I got there.

Next there were seventeen sets of bleachers. Sixteen mistakes later, I was able to crawl under the real one.

It sounded like I'd lost the bad guys. Ah, safe at last. Everything was peaceful and quiet. Well, everything except the pounding in my ears. It had switched from rap music to disco. What was next? Country Western?

And all of this because of one little lie. Why hadn't I just told Wall Street I didn't know what was in the jar? Why did I have to make up that stupid story about nuclear fuel? Sure, it was supposed to be a joke, but right now nobody was laughing . . . especially me.

I wasn't sure what to do, but since it was a warm night, I figured closing my eyes and resting a minute wouldn't hurt.

Before I knew it, I was sound asleep. Next, I was dreaming. Even though I didn't have ol' Betsy to type on, it seemed my subconscious wanted to keep working on the Hydro Dude story. I guess compared to what I was going through in real life, Hydro Dude's adventure seemed kinda peaceful and relaxing.

When we last left Hydro Dude, the dastardly Dr. Yes had just released his deadly toxin into the air, which is vaporizing everything starting with the letter *B*. It's terrible. Everything's going—Baseball Bats, Barbells, Blue Birds. Even all that Broccoli...(well, I guess a little good can come out of any catastrophe).

As he sloshes down the street, Hydro Dude realizes it's worse than he suspects.

—Mothers are screaming, "My Babies, where are my Babies?"
—Landlords are shouting, "My Buildings, where are my Buildings?"
—And health nuts are shrieking, "My Bran muffins, who stole my Bran muffins?"

Now our super-good guy is *really* worried. Is nothing sacred? What's next? Blondes, Bananas, Bathrooms—or worst of all worsts, what about his Thursday Night Bowling League?

Hydro Dude can stand no more. He tilts his fluid head toward the sky and cries, "DR. YES—WHERE ARE YOU? CAN YOU HEAR ME?"

Immediately every radio in every passing car crackles to life. A slith-eringly sinister voice answers, "*YES*."

Hydro Dude has made contact. Now it's time for our clear-as-a-mountain-stream good guy to establish communication. "Are you responsible for all of this?" he asks.

"Yes," comes the answer.

"Are you doing this because you're a misguided bad guy?"

"Yes."

"Is it because you never got enough love at home?"

"Yes."

"Because your parents always said no?"

"Yes."

(Talk about a one-track mind. Does this guy know any other word?)

"And you're doing all this to get my attention so I'll come battle you so you can destroy me?"

"Yes."

So far Hydro Dude is batting a thousand in the lucky guess department. And why not? After all, he's the hero of this story. Besides, that's why they pay him the big superhero bucks. But why does Dr. Yes hate him so? It's just a stab in the dark, but Hydro Dude takes the chance and asks, "Do you hate me because your mom made you learn to do the breast stroke when you were four and a half years old...and you almost drowned...and now you hate anything to do with water?"

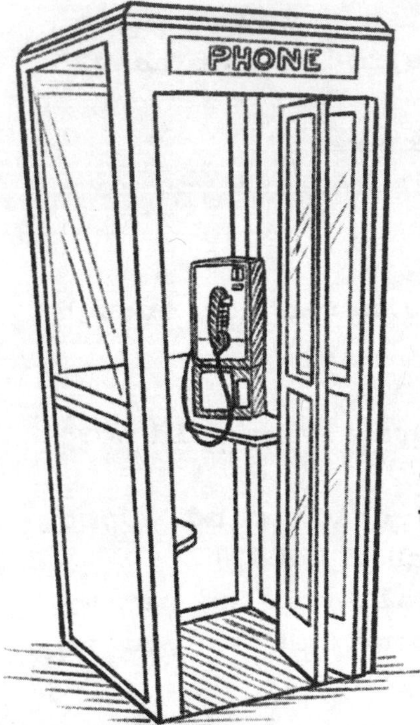

"Yes," the doctor gasps in amazement. (Pretty amazing, huh? Let's see any of your other so-called superheroes top that.)

Quickly Hydro Dude races to an antique phone booth and flips to the bad guys section in the phone book. At last he spots Dr. Yes's advertisement.

DR. YES—SINISTER SLIMEBALL

If You're Looking for

- Unbearable pain
- Heart-stopping terror

or

- Just bad table manners

Dr. Yes Is Your Fiend

Specializing in mass mayhem,
underhanded treachery,
and belching without saying, "Excuse me."
Call for your free estimate today.
Visa and Mastercard accepted.
(Extra charge for thermonuclear war.)

NO ONE CAN SAY "NO" TO YES

Reading the address at the bottom of the page, our hero shouts, "Are you still at your hangout, deep within the bowels of Dodger Stadium?"

"Yes," the doctor answers.

"Then pick up your dirty socks and get ready for some company!"

With that our heroically handsome hero splashes out of the booth and slops onto the jet-powered Harley Davidson that just happens to be idling nearby. In a matter of seconds, he's heading toward Dodger Stadium at 180-don't-try-this-at-home-kids miles per hour.

Everything's going fine as he approaches the stadium's entrance...Well, except the part where his Harley Davidson suddenly vanishes. That's right. You see, although most people know them as motorcycles, other, less refined folks refer to them as motorBikes.

"Yikes!"

Our hero flies into the stadium. "Look, Mom, no hands! Better make that, no bike either!"

He hits the ground and does the world's longest slide into second base...except, of course, there are no longer any Bases. In fact there are no longer any more Baseball stadiums. So instead of sliding along on the nice, soft baseball dirt, Hydro Dude slides along on the not-so-nice, not-so-soft gravel of an unpaved parking lot.

"Double yikes!"

And then he hears it...the sickening rip of his jeans. Oh no! What will he tell his mother? Oh no! Will she take it out of his allowance? Oh no, will she be angry that his liquid body is gushing out of the rip and flowing all over the parking lot?

That's right. Soon, our hero is all over the lot, literally. (Talk about spreading yourself too thin.) Now he

is a twenty-foot-wide puddle that's half an inch tall. He groans, "I guess this ruins my chances of playing for the Lakers."

But there is another problem. The one dealing with the dusty, dry-as-a-bone parking lot. The dusty, dry-as-a-bone parking lot that is already absorbing him—drinking him into its earth.

He groans again, "I guess that also ruins my chances of living."

Chapter 6

Catching a Train

"Attention, please . . . attention."

In my sleep I heard a distant voice and then some major feedback.

SQUEAL!

"Could I have everybody's attention? Attention, please!"

I began to wake up.

"Okay, everybody . . . *SQUEAL* . . . settle down, now. Please settle down."

Before I even opened my eyes, I knew that the voice belonged to Vice Principal Watkins. Nobody in the world can misuse a microphone like that man.

S Q U E A L! (See what I mean?)

I finally pried open my eyes. As far as I could tell, I was still under the bleachers. But now the bleachers were filled with students. What was going on? What were they doing outside?

After throwing in a couple more squeals for good measure, Vice Principal Watkins gave the answer:

"I know we're all under a lot of stress this morning . . ." *SQUEAL*! "We've all seen the news. We all know how one of our beloved students, Wallace McDoogle, has, for some unexplained reason, joined ranks with a terrorist organization."

Kids began to mumble and mutter. I wasn't sure, but I even thought I heard a couple of sniffs and a sob.

Vice Principal Watkins continued, "We're meeting out here because late last night, Wallace was sighted near our school with his container of nuclear material. I've asked the police bomb squad to search the building, to make sure he has not made a bomb and planted it inside."

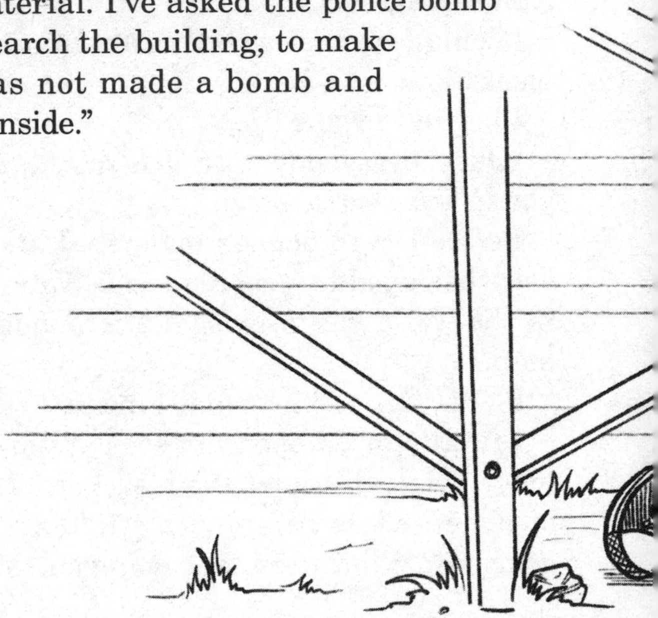

I couldn't believe my ears. For a moment I thought I was still dreaming. But even I couldn't dream up something this crazy.

"I know a lot of you are upset," Vice Principal Watkins continued, "so I've asked Nurse Simpson, a trained professional, to come up and explain how a well-adjusted person, like Wallace, can suddenly snap and go totally berserk."

I rose to my knees. I had to crawl out from under the bleachers and set everything straight. These were my very best friends . . . well, at least we were friends . . . well, okay, so most of them didn't know me from Adam, and those who did always went out of their way to avoid me. But the point is, I was a Dork-oid. And everyone knows Dork-oids aren't clever enough to do the stuff Vice Principal Watkins was saying. If I could just climb out and straighten everything—

"*There he is*!"

I spun around. It was Gary the Gorilla. All seventeen of him. (That's right, I was still wearing my glasses.) Gary and I got to know each other pretty well at Camp "Whacko" last summer. It's not like we became best buds or anything, but at least now he didn't have this uncontrollable urge to smash my face in every time he saw me. He was underneath the bleachers grabbing a smoke with the rest of his goon patrol when he spotted me.

"*He's right here*!" he shouted. "*Wally's right here*!"

Everyone on the bleachers looked underneath. Immediately there were three hundred pairs of eyes all staring down at me—three hundred pairs of eyes that widened in horror as panic swept the crowd.

Nurse Simpson knew it was time to take charge. Being the cool and calm professional she was, she grabbed the microphone and screamed into it at the top of her lungs, "*Somebody grab that fruitcake*! *He's going to blow us all to Jupiter*!"

This didn't help much in the crowd-control department. Everyone began shouting hysterically.

"No," I cried, as I reached for the canister of reddish-pink gunk and held it out. "You don't understand, this is—"

"He's got the bomb with him!" they screamed. "He's going to nuke *us!* We're all going to glow like neon signs!"

Everyone had gone crazy.

I turned to Gary. "You don't understand . . ."

But Gary did understand. He understood it was

time to graduate from being the All-School Bully to becoming the All-School Hero.

He started toward me.

But instead of his usual, bone-breaking threats, he talked sweetly and gently. "Nice Wally, good Wally . . ." He obviously thought that was how you were supposed to treat crazy people—particularly crazy people that can blow you halfway to Jupiter. "Come here, fella, be a good Wally, now, come on, boy. . . ."

I wasn't sure whether to wag my tail or sit up and bark.

Up above, on the bleachers, kids were trampling over one another trying to get away. But Gary paid no attention. He just kept closing in. "Come here, boy, come on now, come on. . . ."

I had to make a decision: let Gary catch me or turn and run for my life. I knew it probably meant I wouldn't be getting any doggie treats, but I voted for the running.

I crawled to the nearest opening in the bleachers and stood. No one noticed. I guess they were all too busy panicking as Nurse Simpson kept screaming, "*Please God . . . I'm too young to die*! *Let me get married, first*! *Please, God, please, God*!"

I wasn't sure where to go. With seventeen hysterical crowds running in seventeen directions, it was kind of tough to make a decision. Suddenly Opera appeared out of the blue and grabbed my arm. "Come on!" he shouted.

Another hand grabbed my other arm. It was Wall Street. "Quick, into the park!"

We raced through the crowd of screaming crazies and finally made it out to the school's sidewalk.

Safe at last.

Well, not exactly. Cindy Cho was in front of the school doing a little on-camera piece. You didn't have to be a rocket scientist to imagine what or *who* she was talking about.

She glanced up and spotted me. "There he is!" she shouted. "It's Wally McDoogle!" She clutched her microphone and yelled to the cameraman. "Come on, let's get him!"

But they'd have to take a number because Gary and his goons were closing in from the other direction. "It's okay, fella, come on, boy. . . ."

Without the help of any crossing guards (we were in kind of a hurry) the three of us raced across the street and into the giant park. Opera and Wall Street did their best to steer me around each of the hundreds of seventeen trees when suddenly Wall Street cried, "What's that sound?"

"I don't hear anything," I said. (An obvious lie, since I was hearing a lot . . . mostly the pounding of my heart.)

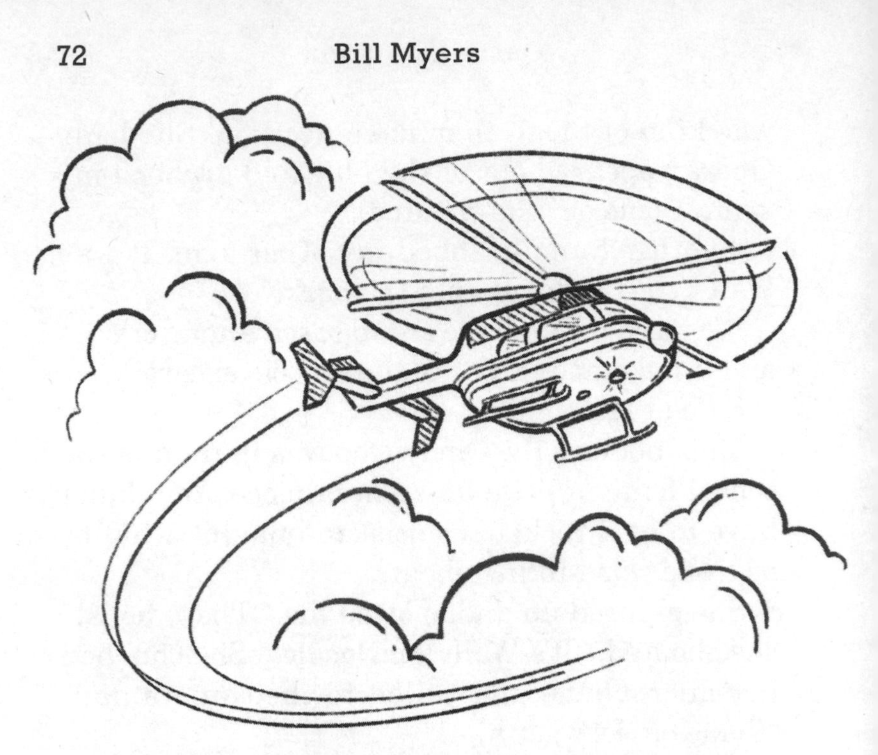

"*Look*!" she pointed toward the sky.

Over the treetops a helicopter appeared. The wind from its rotors kicked up all sorts of dirt and dust. Suddenly a voice boomed: "*Throw down the canister*! *Give yourself up*!"

Opera shouted over the wind. "Who are those guys? Who are they talking to?"

"THROW DOWN THAT CANISTER, McDOOGLE."

Well, that solved half the mystery. We knew who they were talking to, but *who* were *they*?

"Maybe they're the police!" Wall Street shouted.

"Or the real terrorists!" Opera shouted back.

I wasn't sure what to do. Wall Street grabbed my arm and shouted, "Come on!" She pulled us toward the edge of a ravine with lots and lots of bushes. Did I say ravine? It was more like a giant cliff. There were some train tracks halfway down, but the cliff wall was too steep to get to them. I guess she thought we could just hide in the bushes. Not a bad idea, except that the wind from the helicopter squashed everything flatter than a pancake. Everything but us. Soon we were standing out like three Statues of Liberty.

"There they are!" It was Cindy Cho closing in from the right.

"It's okay, fella, you can trust me, boy. . . ." Gary was closing in from the left.

Then, of course, there was the helicopter closing in from overhead.

Suddenly I felt something. A shaking. A rumbling.

"It's the train!" Opera pointed to the tracks halfway down the ravine. "The train is coming!"

We all looked down as a giant freight train slowly ambled by underneath.

"Wally, is there something you'd like to say to the camera?" Cindy was nearly there.

"Easy, fella, easy now. . . ." So was Gary.

Then of course there was the hovering chopper. "*This is your final warning*!"

I looked at Opera and Wall Street. They looked at me. We looked down at the passing train. It was twenty-five feet below. Not far if you're a stunt man, sky diver, or one of my superheroes. But far enough if you're not crazy about broken bones and death.

But it was our only way out.

The boxcars continued to rumble by underneath.

I swallowed hard and shouted, "I hope you all have life insurance."

Wall Street began to smooth down her bangs.

"What are you doing?" Opera shouted.

"If I'm meeting God, I want to look my best."

Opera nodded and started to tuck in his shirttail.

I reached for my glasses and put them in my

pocket. I wasn't sure, but if I saw seventeen trains, did that mean I was going to hit it seventeen times? Next I stuffed the canister of reddish-pink gunk down my shirt.

With a deep breath, we all looked at one another one last time. Then we jumped into the air and . . .

You ever notice how easy it looked when people jump onto things in the movies? They just leaped into the air and, *bingo*, there was their horse, or the frontseat of their convertible, or the bad guy's shoulders.

It was simple, right?

Unfortunately, they never told you how hard it was to actually hit your target. Or the pain you felt if you should actually succeed. Then there was the other problem . . . the one of your body continuing to roll after you had landed.

That was our current challenge.

Hitting the top of the boxcar was fine. Feeling the bone-crushing pain wasn't bad. But rolling across to the other side and falling off . . . well, that was a real bother. The best I remember, it went something like this:

"AHHHHHHHHHHHHHHH!" (That, of course, was our jumping.)

K-BAM! "Boy, that smarts!" (That was our hitting.)

ROLL-ROLL-TUMBLE-TUMBLE!

"AHHHHHHHHHH!!!" (That's our rolling across the roof and plunging over the other side.)

Oh, there was one other sound.

K-RASH! POKE-POKE-POKE, RIP-RIP-RIP!

The best I could make out, we had landed in a giant prickly tree. The good news was it broke our fall before we broke our necks. The bad news was they don't call them "prickly trees" for nothing.

"Ow!" Opera cried.

"My clothes ripped!" Wall Street complained.

"That sure smarts," I moaned.

We all hung from the same branch about ten feet off the ground. The helicopter pounded overhead, but we couldn't see it. Cindy Cho and Gary the Gorilla called from the top of the cliff, but we couldn't see them either.

And since we couldn't see them, I knew they couldn't see us.

"Maybe," I whispered, "if we just hang here real quiet for a while, maybe they'll go away. Maybe they'll think we left. Maybe—"

GROAN!

I looked up at the branch. Maybe Opera shouldn't have eaten so many potato chips.

C R A C K!!

Suddenly the whole branch gave way.

"AHHHHHHHHHHHHHHHHHH!"

The three of us hit the ground about the same

time. Unfortunately, it wasn't any softer than the top of the boxcar. *Unfortunatelier*, it didn't slow us down any more than the top of the boxcar. *Unfortunateliest*, the ravine continued its steep slope downward . . . which meant we continued our little journey downward.

"SPRAAAAKKKKKKK!" (Don't ask me what it means. I was just getting tired of screaming "AHHHHHHH . . ." all the time.)

We rolled and tumbled and fell. And when we got tired of that, we fell and tumbled and rolled. It was a lot of fun—well, except for the blood and bruises part.

After what seemed to be hours, we finally came to a stop at the bottom of the ravine in a bunch of bushes. At first I was mad. It didn't seem fair. I mean, if you're dead, why should you have to keep feeling pain? Then it dawned on me, maybe my luck was worse than I thought. Maybe I was still alive.

Then I heard Opera groaning.

"Opera?" I asked, "Opera, are you here?"

"Barely," he moaned.

"Wall Street?" I looked around. "Is Wall Street with us?"

She raised her hand out of the bushes and groaned, "Present."

I let out a sigh of relief. Well, at least we were all here. True, we may have been a little shaken up, but at least we had lost our pursuers. At least we were safe and sound.

Well, not quite.

Suddenly I heard a familiar woman's voice shouting, "Will you please put away that stupid needlepoint you're doing and see what that noise was!"

I couldn't believe my ears. I raised my head above the bushes. I wished I couldn't believe my eyes. Just to be sure, I reached into my pocket for what was left of my glasses. I slipped them on. Yup, it was just as I thought. We were right next to a gray van hidden under the trees. A gray van that belonged to none other than my Save the Snail buddies.

Chapter 7

A Little House Call

So there we were, lying in the bushes just outside the terrorists' van.

I'll spare you the boring details.

You know, little things like how Big Lug stepped outside to check on the noise. How he couldn't find anything. And then how he lit up a cigarette while standing so close to me that I could count the treads on the bottom of his Nikes.

I won't even talk about the pain when he finished the cigarette and flicked it to the ground (which was actually the back of my hand) and carefully ground it out with his boot. (It gave a whole new meaning to the phrase, *Smoking is hazardous to your health.*)

I won't even mention how he strolled right past Wall Street, stopped to check his pockets for a piece of gum, and accidentally dropped a twenty-dollar bill. From underneath the brush, I could see it flutter to the ground just inches from Wall Street's face.

Poor kid. She lived for making a buck, and now there was an entire fortune right there within sneezing distance. The only problem was Big Lug was also right there, within grabbing distance.

She stared hard at the money, then she glanced over at me through the bushes.

I scowled and mouthed the words, "Don't you dare."

Her eyes darted back to the money, then back to me again. Her face started to twitch—an obvious allergic reaction to having so much money so close.

Big Lug continued to stand directly in front of her, not seeing a thing. Instead, he was looking high into the sky. "You ought to come out here," he called to the woman inside. "The clouds are simply marvelous this time of day."

"Will ya shut up," the woman shouted from inside the van. "I'm trying to watch *General Hospital*."

Wall Street continued staring at the money. By now she'd worked up a pretty good sweat. And still Big Lug stood there, staring at the sky.

A gust of wind tugged at the bill.

Wall Street began to tremble—like one of those drug movies where the addict is trying to kick his habit.

The wind grew stronger. The bill lifted off the ground and started to blow away. Wall Street's eyes widened in horror.

Now, let's face it, there are certain laws in the universe that cannot be changed:

—You spit into the wind; it will come back at you.
—You take a shower; your older brother will freeze you out by flushing the toilet.
—You empty the cat box; the cat will use it within thirty seconds.

These are the cold, hard facts of life. But there's one other:

—You put a twenty-dollar bill under Wall Street's nose and yank it away; you can't blame her for leaping up to try and catch it.

Of course you can't blame Big Lug for grabbing her, either. Which he did. Wall Street kicked and screamed and shouted (I wasn't sure if it was because she wanted to get loose or because the twenty dollars was getting away).

Next Opera decided to get in on the act. Good ol' Opera, what an incredible heart . . . what a tiny brain.

He leaped up and charged at the big guy with all his might.

"You let her go!" he shouted. I suppose my buddy should get an A+ for effort but a definite F- in thinking. Since Big Lug was about five times

Opera's size, it was kinda pathetic—like watching test driver dummies hitting brick walls at sixty miles an hour.

K-BAMB!

But before Opera hit the ground, Big Lug scooped him up with his other hand. Now he had both of my friends, one under each arm.

I had no choice. Too bad. I'd always hoped to get my driver's license before I died. Or at least have my voice change. Then of course, there was my dream of growing to be six-foot-seven-inches tall so I could beat up my older brothers as a return favor for all the poundings I received from them.

Now I would have to give all that up just to save my friends. I carefully hid the jar of gunk in the bushes, then leaped to my feet, and ran at Big Lug with all my strength.

"AUUGGHHHH!"

Big Lug looked at me, kinda perplexed. Then, at the last second, he stepped aside and let me plow into the front of the van directly behind him.

K-RASH!

I staggered backward wondering why there were suddenly so many stars in the middle of the day. Big Lug grabbed me and added me to his kids collection. "Hey!" he shouted to the woman in the van. He opened the door and hauled us inside. "Look what I got."

Anyway, like I said, I won't bore you with all that stuff. Instead, I'll get right to the part where they had the three of us tied up in the van. Big Lug and the woman were grilling us. Behind them, on the dash, was a cell phone streaming something and blaring away.

"So, kid," the woman leaned right into my face, "just tell us where you hid the nuclear stuff you stole."

I answered, "Mumf mruph moomph mumrom."

"What?"

"Mumf mruph moomph mumrom."

"I think he wants you to take the tape off his mouth," Big Lug suggested.

"Oh," the woman said.

RIIIIP!

Yeow! I thought. But, being the courageous type I am, I didn't show my pain. Oh no. Instead, I opened my mouth and said something heroic like, "Oh, please, please don't hurt us. I beg you, please. We didn't do anything. Please, please! I don't know what nuclear stuff you're talking about. Please, there's been a horrible mistake. Please, please, please . . ." You know, something manly like that.

But the woman didn't buy it. "Don't play the ignorant coward with me," she said.

Who's playing? I thought.

"We know you have the nuclear material," she sneered, "and we know that another terrorist organization is after it."

It was time to muster up all of my McDoogle intelligence and hit her with my stunning brain power. "Huh?" I said.

"We heard it on the police scanner," she answered. "You called up your accomplice," she pointed at Wall Street, "and told her about the nuclear material and the terrorists who had called for it."

"But that was just a joke," I croaked.

"A joke?"

"Yeah, a lie. You see, me and Opera, we'd been practicing lying all day long. We just called up Wall Street and pretended—"

Big Lug interrupted. "Nice try, McDoogle, but we saw your folks on the news. They said you go to Sunday school and everything."

"So?"

"So you know that telling lies is wrong, and you wouldn't do something like that."

My mouth dropped open. I wanted to ask him what planet he was visiting from. That just because something was wrong didn't mean I wasn't stupid enough to try it. I wanted to say all that, but the only thing that came out was, "But . . ."

"But, what?" Big Lug asked.

"But, but . . ."

"But, but, what?" he repeated.

"But, but, but—"

"Shhh," the woman waved for us to be quiet and pointed to the cell phone on the dash. It was Cindy Cho again. She had late-breaking news.

**"Day Two—Wally McDoogle,
Terrorist at Large"**

I threw a look over to Opera and Wall Street. They rolled their eyes in perfect unison.

Back on the news feed they showed the three of us jumping off the cliff onto the moving boxcar. It looked pretty impressive, except the part where we rolled off the other side screaming for our lives.

Next they showed footage of the National Guard being called into action—some soldiers and a helicopter. The helicopter looked a lot like the one that had tried to get me to throw down the canister.

Oh, brother, I thought. *It can't get any worse than this.*

As usual I was wrong.

The governor of the state was on the news. That's right, Mr. Big himself. He was giving some sort of statement to the press. Something about taking whatever measures necessary to stop the spread of terrorist activity within our borders. He didn't mention me by name, but it was pretty obvious who he had in mind.

Suddenly came the explosion. At first I thought it was my heart leaping out of my chest. (Which was okay—a nice heart attack about now would have been a welcomed relief.)

But it wasn't.

It was Gary and his gang. They broke down the van door and stormed inside. Before Big Lug or the woman could stop him, Gary and his goons had thrown them to the back of the van.

Gary reached for my ropes and quickly untied me. "Nice Wally, good fellow. Yes, you're a good boy . . ."

"*Look out*!" Opera shouted, "*She's got a gun*!"

We spun around to see that the woman had grabbed her shotgun.

Now, the way I figured it, once again I had two choices. I could race out the door and run like crazy, or stick around and become McDoogle Swiss Cheese (with little shotgun pellet ventilation holes).

Since I was allergic to dairy products and to being killed, I again voted for running like crazy.

"AHHHHHHHHHHH!"

That was me jumping out the door.

SWOOSH!

I swooped up the canister I'd hidden in the bushes.

KR-THUD!

I hit another one of the seventeen trees in front of me. (I definitely needed to get those glasses fixed.)

I staggered backward, seeing even more stars than before. But, somehow, I was able to keep my balance and resume my little escape.

Big Lug and the woman jumped out of the back. They were followed by Opera and Wall Street. But they weren't my only fans. Up above on the hill, I noticed Cindy Cho and her cameraman climbing down. "There he is! Get a close-up, get a close-up!"

Above my head the National Guard helicopter reappeared.

THUMP, THUMP, THUMP.

And of course there was Gary the Gorilla saying, “Come here, Wally, come on. Good boy, come on, fella . . .”

I was surrounded. There was no place to go. Well, not exactly.

Chapter 8

Photo Opportunities

I raced down the path. Luckily, I knew the park like the back of my hand. (Well, the back of my hand before Big Lug smashed his cigarette out on it.) I took a turn to the left and found myself in the bandstand area. This was where outdoor concerts were performed. I raced past the empty seats and hopped up on the stage. I had to find someplace, anyplace to hide. Then I saw it—a little trapdoor in the stage near the front.

Perfect.

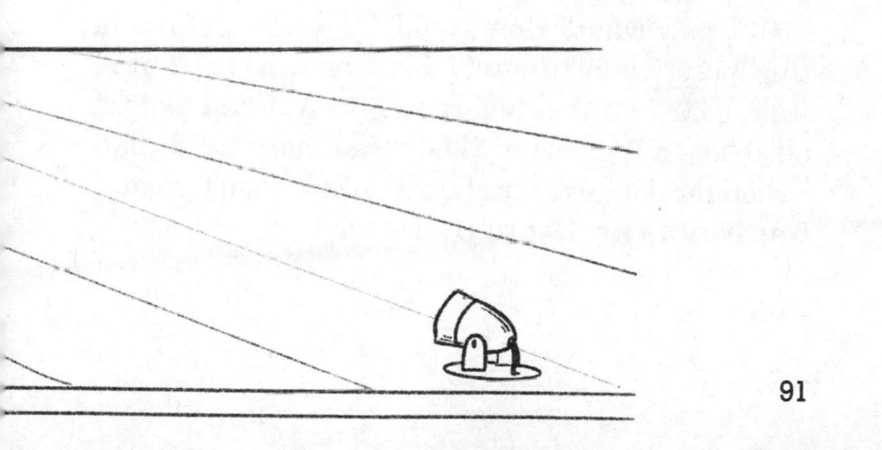

I squeezed down through the opening until I was underneath the stage. No one could possibly find me there.

For once I was right.

Big Lug and the woman raced by. Although they couldn't see, they kept shouting: "Wally, think of our cause, think of those poor suffering snails . . . "

Then Cindy Cho: "Wally, I can get you on national TV with Tom Brokenoff!"

Then the helicopter: *THUMP, THUMP, THUMP!*

And, of course, Gary: "Here, Wally, here, boy, here, boy."

At last their voices started to fade. Good. They were gone. Part of me wanted to climb back up on the stage and get out of there, but part of me just wanted to rest and think things through.

It was hard to believe. So much had happened in just twenty-four hours . . . all because of a stupid lie. I tell you, if God were trying to tell me something, I was starting to get the point.

But now what? How could I possibly get out of this mess? Unfortunately, I had no time to think. I was so bushed that before I knew it, I had drifted off to sleep. I guess my body was more tired than I thought. Unfortunately, my mind wasn't. Soon I was back to my Hydro Dude story.

When we last left our lovable liquid, he had spilled out of the rip in his jeans and was being absorbed into the dirt of a giant parking lot. Oh no! What will he do? How will he survive? How will he get back in time to do his complex fractions homework? (Oh, well, every cloud has its silver lining.)

But it isn't over for Hydro Dude—not by a long squirt. With superior super-dude effort, he sucks and siphons and slurps himself back into his clothes, ties knots in the holes, and once again stands tall and straight.

But he is unable to rid himself of the dirt his liquid body has absorbed. He is no longer the super-clean, super-clear fluid. And since superheroes always have super-accurate names (it's in their Good-Guy contract), he knows he can no longer be called Hydro Dude.

Instead, he quickly comes up with a new name. No longer is he Hydro Dude, but...Da-Da-Daaaaa...(that's superhero intro music)...he is now: Mud Man.

Faster than a speeding car wash. Able to leap upon white pants in a single splash. Look! Up in the sky! It's a bird. It's a plane. It's KERSPLAT... Mud Man!

Ol' Muddy squishes forward. Dr. Yes is still on the loose and must be stopped before he rids the world of everything starting with the letter *B*.

Our hero shouts, "Dr. Yes! Dr. Yes, are you here?"

The answer comes from directly behind him.

"Yes." (So what'd you expect..."No"?)

Mud Man spins around as the dastardly Dr. Yes rushes at him with a bar of soap. The gleam in the doctor's eyes says he has only one thing on his mind.

Mud Man sees it and cries, "So, you think you'll wash me away?"

"Yes!" the doctor screams.

"That you'll clean up my act?"

"Yes!"

"That I'm all washed up?" (We could go on like this forever, but you're probably getting the idea.)

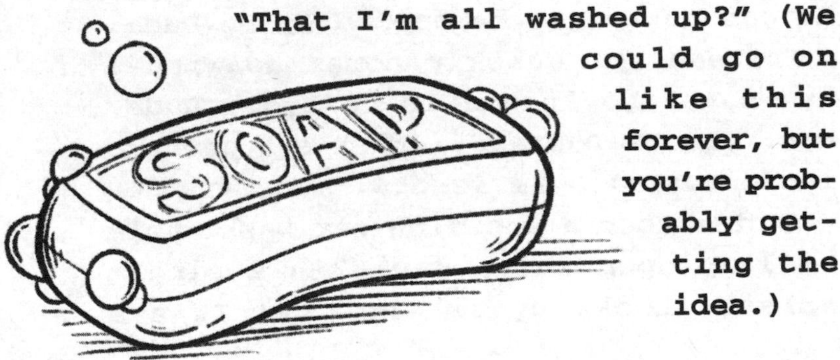

Mud Man tries to grab the soap from the doctor and shouts, "It won't be that easy to wash your hands of me!" (Sorry, I had to get one more in.)

They begin to fight. Back and forth. Forth and back. It's a deadly dance. Soon they're doing a Waltz, then the Foxtrot, now the Twist. Bubbles and suds are everywhere. I mean, these guys are really working themselves up into... (here it comes)...a lather. (Hey, what's an extra bad joke between friends?)

"You will not destroy me!" Mud Man cries.

"Yes!" Dr. Yes shouts. "Yes! Yes! Yes! Yes!" (As you may have noticed ol' Doc's a little short on vocabulary.)

Soon, Mud Man's super-strength overwhelms the dastardly Doc. But, just when it looks like our hero's won the day, Dr. Yes reaches down to his Secret Gadgetron Belt—sold at bad-guy stores everywhere—and presses a button.

FIZZLE, CRACKLE, BLEEP, BOP...BURP.

Suddenly, in front of their very eyes, a small car with a giant drill attached to the front appears. Oh, no! It's Dr. Yes's famous Mole Mobile!

Before you can say, "Isn't this just a little too convenient?" Dr. Yes slips out of Mud Man's hands and hops into the cockpit of the Mole Mobile. He quickly switches switches, dials dials, and, uh, buttons buttons.

GROAN, CREAK, COUGH-COUGH-COUGH, WHEEZE!

Nothing happens. The battery is deader than a jack rabbit after losing at tag with a semi. He tries again.

GROAN, CREAK, COUGH, K-PUTT, K-PUTT, K-PUTT-PUTT-PUTT-PUTT!

Soon the giant drill bit in the front begins to turn...faster and faster and faster some more.

Mud Man's jaw drops open in amazement as the Mole Mobile spins around and races at him. Realizing Dr. Yes's drill is aiming directly for his open mouth. Mud Man leaps aside and shouts, "No thanks, I have my own dentist!"

Being the quick-thinking superhero he is, Mud Man jumps on top of the spinning drill, which sends him twirling out of control. "WHOA—WAAA—WOOO!"

(Hey, I said he was quick-thinking, not smart.)

Fortunately, the ride is short-lived. He's flung aside like a giant mud pie—*KR-SPLASH!*

He raises his mud head and watches in amazement as the Mole Mobile rises up on its back wheels and points directly into the dirt. Its drill nose bores into the ground until the entire machine is tunneling its way through the earth.

In another flash of superhero thinking—this time a little smarter than the last—Mud Man kicks off his shoes and slowly oozes back out of his pant legs.

It is going to be tricky, but the only way to stop this baddest of bad guys is for Mud Man to once again return to his super-fluid form. Hopefully, he can flow through the ground faster than the sun can evaporate him. Hopefully, he can leave the mud behind and again become Hydro Dude. Hopefully, he won't run across some groundhog that suddenly thinks it's time for a good long drink.

Suddenly Hydro Dude hears beautiful music. Suddenly he hears people clapping. Suddenly he feels the ground starting to rise. Suddenly...

I woke up. When I had dozed off, I was all safe and secure below the trapdoor opening of the stage. No people. No noise. But someone had pressed a button, and now my little section of stage was rising up through the trapdoor. Higher and higher I rose. Louder and louder the music grew.

Soon, my head popped up, then my shoulders, then the rest of the body. There I was: standing right in the center of a Middletown Symphony Orchestra performance. The conductor didn't look happy about seeing me. Come to think of it, the musicians weren't too thrilled either.

Then, of course, there were the nine gazillion people sitting in the audience. Nine gazillion people all staring at me. "It's Wally McDoogle!" someone shouted. "The boy with the bomb!"

I glanced down at my hand. Sure enough, I was still holding the infamous canister of gunk.

Security guards appeared at both ends of the stage. They raced toward me. One of them was already on his cell phone, which meant I'd soon be seeing my buddies from the National Guard, the TV station, and the rest of the old gang. I could hardly wait.

I was blinded by *FLASH, FLASH, FLASH!*

A bunch of flashes were going off. I looked into the audience. There must have been two dozen tourists in the first couple of rows taking pictures and videos of America's newest and most-talked-about tourist attraction.

Me!

FLASH, FLASH, FLASH!

I half-leaped and half-fell off the stage.

FLASH, FLASH, FLASH!

I scrambled to my feet. What now? Where could I go? Where could I take this troublesome canister of gunk so people would leave me alone?

Then I had it. The museum! Of course! That's where this had all started. That's where I got the canister in the first place. I'd just return it where I found it and everything would go back to normal, right?

(Okay, so my life had never exactly been normal, but everybody could dream.)

I started down the path.

By now it was pretty dark. But since the tourists decided to follow . . . *FLASH, FLASH, FLASH!* . . . I had plenty of light to show me the way. Finally I came to the park entrance.

Over at the curb, a city bus was boarding passengers. I raced to it, jumped inside, and slid into the nearest seat just as the bus doors hissed shut. Whew, that was close.

Unfortunately, not close enough.

The bus doors hissed open again. It looked like somebody else wanted on. But it wasn't just one somebody else, it was two dozen somebody elses.

FLASH, FLASH, FLASH!

Two dozen somebody elses with cameras and cell phones, all wanting to take pictures of themselves sitting next to the most feared gangster of all time to show their friends back home.

Sigh.

Suddenly the bus driver recognized me and was shaking like a leaf. Unable to take his eyes from the canister he cried, "P-p-please, don't blow us up, M-M-Mr. McDoogle."

"I won't hurt you!" I shouted over the whirring videos and flashing. "Where does this bus go?"

"Anywhere y-y-you want it to, s-s-sir."

"How 'bout the Museum of Natural History?"

He nodded and quickly threw the bus into gear. We were on our way.

It wasn't long before I heard the old familiar *THUMP, THUMP, THUMP*. I craned my neck against the window and looked up. Sure enough, it was my buddies from the National Guard.

Next came a squeal of tires. I glanced to the left and saw my favorite terrorists pulling up in their van. Then another squeal of tires on the other side, and there was Cindy Cho and WART-TV. And what headache would be complete without a couple of SWAT trucks pulling up from behind? (I just love parades, don't you?)

We rounded the final corner and there was the museum. Good. Don't get me wrong, I loved hanging out with all my new tourist friends, but I was getting a bad case of writer's cramp from signing all the autographs. So when the doors hissed open, I said good-bye, jumped off the bus, and ran toward the museum. Of course, there were the usual:

"Throw down that bomb!"

"Save the Snails!"

"Do you have any statement for the press?!"

"Here, Wally; come on, fella; be a good boy . . ."

I was surprised to hear Gary's voice in the choir, but I guess good news travels fast.

I threw open the front door to the museum and was met with the normal screaming hysteria.

"It's Madman McDoogle! He's going to blow us all to smithereens!"

I raced down the hall toward the Dinosaur Exhibit. But when I got there the doors were locked.

By now I could hear the pitter-patter of feet—SWAT feet, news feet, terrorist feet, tourist feet. Yes, sir, it was turning into a regular tap-dance convention.

Then I spotted the stairway. I darted to the steps and took them three at a time. Well, I was hoping to take them three at a time. Most of the time I was taking them none at a time—doing my basic slip-and-fall-and-slip-some-more routine.

Directly behind me I heard a woman, "OOAF, you clumsy—OWW, those are my—WILL YOU WATCH IT!"

"I can't see a thing in these tacky, non-designer, ski masks."

I didn't have to look. I knew my terrorists buddies were close behind.

Somehow I made it to the top of the stairs. Up ahead was a door marked "Balcony."

I ran to it, grabbed the door, and threw it open.

K-BAMB!

(When you're throwing open doors, it's best to step back so you don't smash in your face.)

I made a mental note for the next time, and staggered onto the balcony. Below me was *Tyrannosaurus Rex*, looking better than ever. In the thirty-two hours we'd been apart they'd managed to get her glued back together.

Great.

What was not so great was the two terrorists right behind me. "Hand it over, McDoogle! Join our cause!"

What was even less great was Gary and his buddies throwing open the door at the other end of the balcony. "Here, Wally; good boy; come on now . . . "

I was trapped. There was nowhere to go, and the main floor was a good thirty (that's-sure-going-to-smart-if-I-jump) feet below.

Then I spotted it: the firehose.

I don't know if I'd seen it on TV or written about it in one of my superhero stories. But I grabbed the hose, slipped the reddish-pink gunk under my arm, and leaped over the edge.

"AHHHHHHHhhhhhh . . . "

It was a great jump . . . beautiful . . . stupendous . . . except for one little problem.

The balcony was 30-feet high, and the hose was

100-feet long. Unfortunately I didn't realize this until I was in midair. I'm no mathematician, but the way I figured it, with 100 feet of hose and only a 30-foot drop, I'd still have an extra 70 feet of hose to spare when I smashed myself to death on the floor.

I just hate math, don't you?

But then, just before I crashed into the floor, just before I turned myself into a McDoogle omelet, the hose gave a giant jerk and I stopped. For some unexplained reason, I was hanging halfway between the balcony and the floor.

I clung to the hose looking around. And then I saw it. Ol' Rexy had caught me. My hose had wrapped around her teeth and jaw and was stuck. I couldn't believe it! I was safe! What a break! What a miracle!

The doors below burst open and everyone poured in.

What a bummer.

So there I was hanging above the SWAT guys, Cindy Cho, her cameraman, and two dozen . . .

FLASH, FLASH, FLASH . . . tourists.

I threw a look back up to Rexy. She was still holding my slender thread of a hose between her teeth.

I should have been grateful, but all I could do was think . . . *So this is it. It figures. My whole existence reduced to this. My whole life becoming nothing more than dinosaur dental floss.*

Chapter 9

News Conference

So there I was, hanging above everybody like a human piñata. (I just hoped they wouldn't be passing out sticks and trying to break me open for candy.) Above me were Gary, his goon patrol, and, of course, my old pals the terrorists. Below me the SWAT guys were in position with their rifles, Cindy Cho was in position with her camera, and the tourists were in position with their *FLASH, FLASH, FLASH!*

But not for long. Just when I thought things couldn't possibly get any worse, they got, well, you're probably used to this now, after all I am Wally McDoogle.

"It's bubbling!" somebody shouted. "His nuclear fuel—it's bubbling."

I glanced to the canister under my arm. Sure enough. The gunk was starting to bubble—probably from all the bouncing and shaking it was getting.

"It's going to blow!" a guard shouted. "Let's get out of here! It's going to blow!"

Suddenly everyone and their brother (and a few sisters, I imagine) went into major panic. They raced toward the doors screaming, "Help us! Help us! We're going to die! We're going to die!"

In a matter of seconds the room was empty—well, except for me and Rexy girl. I'm sure she would have gone too, but she'd already done the dying bit (quite a few years back), and her feet were bolted to the ground. And me? Well, like I said, I was kinda hung up at the moment.

Finally I shouted, "Excuse me? Can anybody help me? Hello?" Talk about feeling rejected. Here I was, the life of the party, and suddenly there was no party.

My arms were aching. I couldn't hang onto the hose much longer. I thought about dropping and hitting the floor, but I hesitated. The drop wouldn't be the problem. The "hitting the floor" might be. Not so much for me—hey, I'm used to a broken bone from time to time—but the crash might be a problem for the nuclear stuff. A little smashing into the floor is all it might take to blow up.

I looked over my shoulder and noticed Cindy Cho and her cameraman inching back in. Only now they were wearing radiation suits, like in those science fiction movies. Good ol' Cindy—always prepared. I figured she'd come back to help me, to encourage me, to share stirring words of inspiration.

"Excuse me, Wally," she asked, "do you have any last words to the nation before you get vaporized?"

It was time to show what I was made of. Time to take my medicine like a man, to be brave, heroic, and, above all, strong. "*I* didn't do it!" I screamed. "Please, it's all a mistake! A big lie! I picked this jar up by accident. I'm not trying to hurt anybody!"

Cindy looked a little on the disappointed side. "You mean . . . you just found that canister? You're not a terrorist?"

"That's right."

"Then . . . " She swallowed hard, almost afraid to ask the next question. "Then, you're really not trying to blow up the world?"

I nodded so hard I almost got whiplash.

She sighed heavily and muttered, "So much for the Pulitzer."

My arms had no more strength. They were jelly. It was a matter of seconds before I'd crash to the floor and blow us up. But suddenly, to my rescue, a dozen men wearing something like space suits stormed into the room. They carried all sorts of gizmos and gadgets—scientific junk that I didn't recognize.

What they didn't carry was what I needed. A ladder.

"Uh, fellas . . . I can't hang on any longer."

No answer. Just a lot of beeps and bops as they turned on their equipment and pointed it at me.

Well, it was fun while it lasted. My hands started slipping. My heart started pounding. My lips started praying.

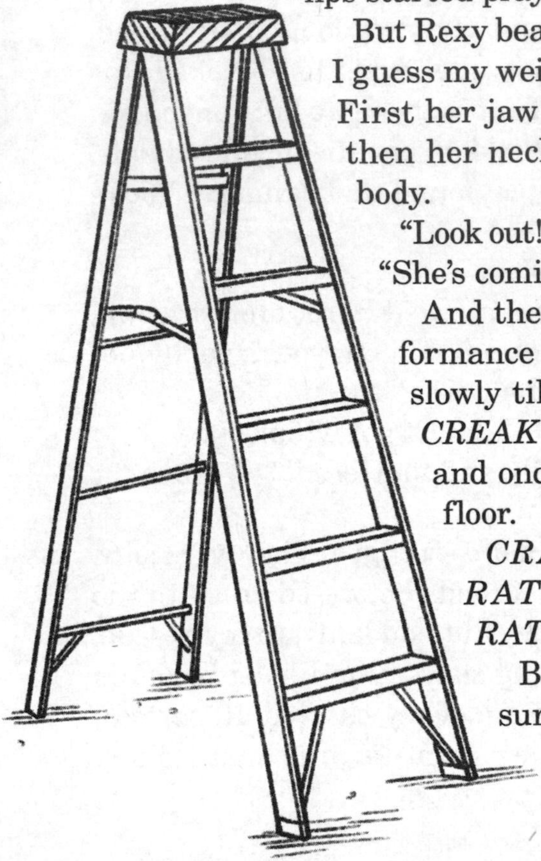

But Rexy beat me to the punch. I guess my weight was too much. First her jaw started to creak, then her neck, then her whole body.

"Look out!" someone shouted. "She's coming down again!"

And then, in a repeat performance of yesterday, Rexy slowly tilted, gave one last *CREAK* for old time's sake, and once again fell to the floor.

CRASH, RUMBLE, RATTLE, RATTLE, RATTLE!

But to everyone's surprise there was no *K-BOOOOOM!*

Just the sound of bones falling and a couple of "AUGGHHHHHs" and "OUCHes" and a "BOY THAT SMARTS" from me.

I was covered in bones as I looked to the canister in amazement. There were still a few bubbles from all the shaking, but it hadn't blown.

Incredible.

It took a little doing, but I finally scrambled up through the pile of bones until I reached the top and could look around. Poor Rexy. Talk about needing a good chiropractor.

Without a word I sort of half-slid, half-fell down Bone Mountain until I reached the floor. Whew, safe at last.

Dream on . . .

When I reached the bottom, I noticed no one was waiting to greet me. No keys to the city, no marching bands, not even a handshake. Instead, everyone had formed a giant circle as they kept pointing their gadgets and recording their data.

"Who are you people?" I asked.

The head guy punched his intercom button and spoke through a small speaker in his helmet. "We're from the Nuclear Regulatory Commission."

I'm sure that was supposed to mean something, but at the moment I was in your basic clueless mode.

Everybody continued their readings. A couple of them shouted out some measurements that made no sense to me but put a frown on Head Guy's face.

"What's wrong?" I asked.

"Whatever that stuff is," he pointed to the canister of gunk, "I've never seen anything like it. Currently there is no reading of radiation, but still . . ." He dropped off as he checked his own meters and gauges.

I started to cross to him, holding out the canister. "Here," I said, "you want to take a better look at—"

"No!" he looked up startled and quickly stepped back. Everyone in the room followed his lead. Soon they were all against the wall, as far from me as possible.

I hesitated a moment and then smiled in understanding. Of course, it had been a good thirty-six hours since I'd showered or brushed my teeth.

But that wasn't the problem. Head Guy cleared his throat. "Please, keep that, that," he motioned toward my jar, "whatever it is, keep it away."

I looked at the canister. "You mean you're afraid you might get contaminated?"

The man held my eyes a moment and then nodded.

The seriousness of his answer slowly sank in. They had on those fancy suits and were still worried about getting contaminated, and I was just wearing my thrashed clothes.

Somehow I felt I knew the answer to my next question, but I still had to ask. "What . . . what about me?"

Silence hung over the room. Finally Head Guy spoke. "I'm sorry, Mr. McDoogle, you have already been exposed to its contents."

I looked back to the canister and nodded. "So . . . so, what do I do now?"

Head Guy hesitated, then said, "Your country needs your help, Mr. McDoogle. We need you to—"

Suddenly another fellow in another space suit raced into the room. In his hand was a cellphone. "It's the president!" he shouted as he crossed to Head Guy. "The president wants to talk to you."

Head Guy glanced to me then reached for the phone.

"Yes, Mr. President?" He listened a moment.

I looked around the circle. "The president of what?" I asked.

The serious look on everyone's face gave me my answer.

Head Guy continued his conversation. "Yes, sir, that's correct. No, sir, I was about to tell him. Yes, sir, he's right here."

Without another word, he lowered the phone, looked at me, and took several cautious steps forward. I watched as he set the phone on the floor and then quickly headed back to the wall.

I looked to the phone, then up to him. "For me?" I squeaked.

Head Guy nodded gravely.

I stood there a moment, not believing what was happening. After a moment I was able to find my legs. I slowly walked toward the phone. I stumbled over a couple of stray Rexy bones along the way, but at last I arrived. There was the President of the United States—waiting to talk to me. Me, Wally If-It-Can-Go-Wrong-You-Can-Bet-It-Will McDoogle.

I heard Cindy Cho whisper to her cameraman, "We've got a national feed; we're going live. Hit it." The camera's light flared on.

I carefully stooped down and picked up the

phone. It was time to use all of my intelligence and muster up all of my composure. I cleared my throat and calmly screamed: "It wasn't my fault. I just found it lying around here. And if you want to blame someone, find the guy that—"

"Uh, Mr. McDoogle?" he interrupted.

"Yes, sir?" I croaked.

"May I call you Wally?"

"You can call me anything you like, although a lot of my friends call me a Dork-oid, but they're really not my friends because I don't have that many, unless you count Wall Street and Opera. But they're Dork-oids too, so—"

"Uh, Wally?"

"Yes, sir?"

"I'm sure that's all very important, but your country has a tremendous request to make of you."

"My country, sir?"

"Yes, Wally. I understand that this was all a giant mix-up and you really had nothing to do with stealing the canister."

"Yes, sir."

"But the fact of the matter is, you are the one who has been exposed."

"Yes, sir." I glanced at the jar. "I guess I am."

"Now, some people say I'm calling you because it's an election year and I want higher ratings in the polls."

I glanced to Cindy Cho. She was motioning for another close-up.

He continued. “There is not an ounce of truth to that accusation. However, if I am re-elected president, I want all of my fellow Americans out there to know that, unlike my opponent, I will balance the budget, increase employment, boost our sagging economy, care for the environment, and furthermore—”

“Uh, Mr. President?” It was my turn to interrupt. “You wanted me to do something?”

“Oh, yes.” He paused a second, then continued. “Wally—it’s a great risk I’m asking you to take, but you are the only one who can discard that nuclear material. You are the only one who can take it to a disposal site before it blows up.”

“But what if I’m too late?” I asked, glancing at the jar. “What if it blows up while I’m carrying it?”

There was another pause. Finally the answer. “What if I promise we’ll make a nice bronze statue of you, will that help?”

“A statue of *me*?”

“Yes.”

Wow! I thought. *There I’d be, standing in some park with people from all around the world coming to look up at me. Children would tell their children, their grandchildren, their great-grandchildren all about my famous McDoogle courage. (Of course*

I'd be deader than a doornail, so I wouldn't be around to hear them. But, hey, every plan has its drawbacks.)

There was, however, one drawback I couldn't get over. I'd seen it with a hundred statues in a hundred parks, and I had to ask.

"Mr. President?"

"Yes, Wally?"

"What about pigeon poop?"

"Pardon me?"

"You know," I explained, "famous statues of famous people always have pigeon poop on them. I mean, I wouldn't want any statue of me to be standing around with a bunch of pigeon—"

"All right, I get the picture," he interrupted. I heard him cover up the phone and talk to someone—obviously some high-ranking official. Finally he spoke back into the phone, "Okay . . . we'll not only make a nice statue of you, but we will assign someone to hose it down at the end of every day. How's that sound? Do we have a deal?"

What did I have to lose? I mean, besides being exposed to deadly radioactivity, being blown to kingdom come, turning into a human mushroom cloud, and missing out on my next eighty or so birthdays, it sounded like a pretty cool deal.

And then, just before I was about to make history, just before I was to lay down my life for my country, a strange man in overalls and a baseball cap burst through the doors.

"Nice work," he shouted as he glanced at the pile of bones behind me. "I see you've been visiting our dinosaur exhibit again."

He pushed his way through the line of space suits and headed directly for me. Everyone gasped, but nobody moved to stop him. They were too stunned.

"What are you doing?" I cried. "Don't you know what I'm holding in my hand?"

"I sure do," he said. "It's my Aunt Zelda's rhubarb sauce."

"What?!"

"I guess in all the confusion yesterday, our lunch sacks got mixed up—you got mine and I got yours." He held out my old lunch sack. "Here you go."

I couldn't move. I was frozen in disbelief. "Rhubarb sauce?" I stammered.

"You betcha," he said, as he took the canister out of my hand and replaced it with my sack. "She makes the best rhubarb sauce in the county—maybe the whole state."

By the look on my face, he could tell I wasn't buying it. In fact, no one in the room was buying it. So, to prove his point, he unscrewed the lid. It was on pretty tight, but at last he pried it off. Next, he reached into his overalls pocket, pulled out a plastic spoon, and dug in. Everyone held their breath as he took the first bite.

Everyone but him. He sighed in contentment. "Ahhh . . . wonderful." Then, offering me a spoonful, he asked, "Wanna try?"

"Ah, no thanks."

He shrugged. "Suit yourself."

After a couple more bites he screwed the lid back onto the container, wiped off the spoon, and crammed both of them into his overalls pocket. "Well, you have a nice evening, now," he smiled. "And thanks for hanging on to this for me."

I sort of nodded as he turned, tipped his cap to the space suit guys, and headed out the door.

There was a long moment as we all stood in silence. I looked around the room—at the pile of dinosaur bones, the men in their space suits, and Cindy Cho with her national feed.

Suddenly I remembered the president. I turned back to the phone, cleared my voice, and said, "Sir, does this mean I won't be getting my statue?"

Chapter 10

Wrapping Up

There you have it. That's how one little lie grew and grew and *grew some* more. Get it? "Grew some" . . . "gruesome." Okay, fine, so I'm no comedian. Big deal.

The point is I learned my lesson. No more lying, no more exaggerating, no more tall tales . . . unless, of course, I become a famous writer, then everybody will pay me lots of money to make up outrageous things like this.

Go figure.

Of course, there were a few little details that needed taking care of.

Like getting Rexy put back together. Basically, the museum figured if you totally destroy a dinosaur once in your life, it's okay. But to do it twice within thirty-two hours, well, they definitely get a little touchy about it.

Luckily, Mom and Dad came to my rescue.

Sort of. Instead of having me sent to prison, they had me work for the museum after school and on weekends until everything was paid back. Not a bad deal—except I won't be done until sometime in the year 3043.

Then there's my Save the Snail buddies. Of course, they got arrested, and of course, the judge threw the book at them for kidnapping me. I don't know how long they'll be in jail, but I figure the snails better keep their heads low because it's

going to be a long time before anybody comes to their rescue.

As usual, Wall Street tried to make a financial killing off my misfortune. She wanted to buy the dinosaur bones and have me autograph them to sell to tourists around the world. But the museum said no, so she tried it with chicken bones. It wasn't much of a success. Ever try autographing chicken bones?

Now she's teaming up with Opera to open up a chain of rhubarb-sauce restaurants. Chips and

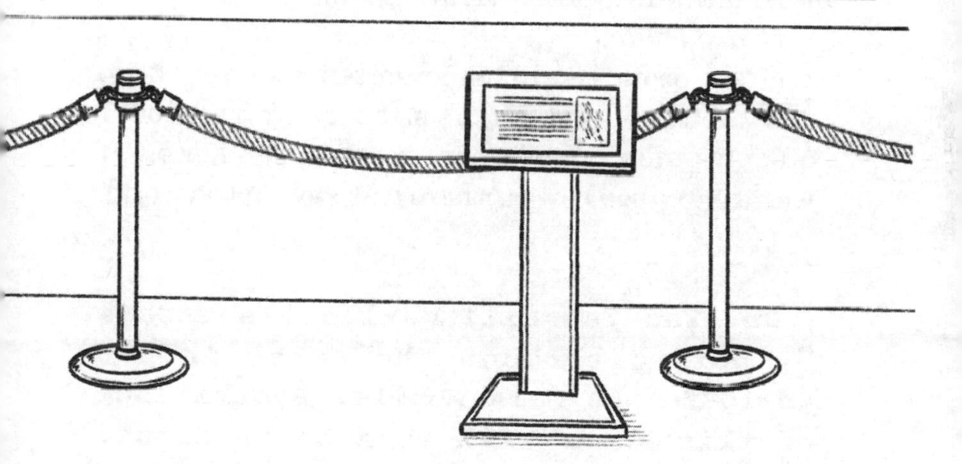

Barb they're calling it. (The chips were Opera's idea.) You sure can't fault them for trying. (Maybe for not having a brain, but definitely not for trying.)

Then there's Cindy Cho. I don't want to say her boss was upset that she spent a whole twenty-four hours on a wild-goose chase, but the last time I saw her, she was doing the weather for the 11:00 p.m. news on a local cable channel.

And finally there's Gary the Gorilla. To hear him tell the story, you'd think he was the one who saved the day. But I'm not going to argue. When a guy's five foot eleven and all muscle, he can be the hero of anything he wants, any time he wants, any way he wants. I just wish when he passes me in the halls he would stop patting me on the head and saying, "Good, Wally; that's a nice boy."

And finally, there's Hydro Dude.

Hydro Dude!

Great Scott, I'd almost forgotten about my little story. After a good night's sleep in my own bed, I quickly pulled out ol' Betsy and snapped her on. It was time to see how our hero was saving the world.

Dr. Yes is still making his escape by boring through the earth in his world-famous Mole Mobile. By the look of things, he will soon be in China.

But do not fear, Hydro Dude will stop him before he arrives. After all, Hydro Dude hates Chinese food. It's not the food, really; it's the chopsticks. He's never gotten the hang of 'em. Especially the soup part—how can anybody eat soup with chopsticks?

Unfortunately, such mysteries must wait for another story, because at this exact moment Dr. Yes is still vaporizing everything that starts with the letter *B*.

Our hydraulic hero flows through the rocks at record speed until he reaches the Mole Mobile and slips in through the open window.

"Give it up!" our hero shouts as he splashes all over Dr. Yes's face, shoulders, and arms. "I've got you covered."

The doctor does not respond, but he quickly shifts his Mole Mobile into This-Is-as-Fast-as-She-Goes. They bore through the earth at an even greater speed.

Suddenly for no explained reason (except the one you'll figure out in just a moment), the drill Bit on the Mole Mobile disappears.

Next, the Boulders he is burrowing through are gone!

Next, he is no longer Burrowing at all!

But, strangest of all stranges, the Mole Mobile is no longer Below. It has returned to the surface of the earth.

"What's happening?" Hydro Dude shouts.

(Of course, being the intelligent reader you are, you could tell him, but you won't...unless, of course, you want to hurry and finish this up so you can watch TV.)

In any case, Dr. Yes finally shuts down the Mole Mobile.

PUTT-PUTT-COUGH-WHEEZE-GASP!

"Wait a minute!" Hydro Dude shouts. "I get it. We're back on the surface because I'm such a super superhero that I saved the day without even knowing how I did it!"

Dr. Yes rolls his eyes and shakes his head.

(You really can't blame Hydro Dude for being so stupid. After all, he only has water for a brain.)

And then, suddenly, it hits our hero like a load of Bricks (it would have been a "load of bricks," but since there are no *Bs*...well, you probably get the picture). "I understand now," he shouts. "We aren't 'Below' because 'Below' starts with the letter *B*!"

"Give the man a prize," Dr. Yes sneers. "But I'm afraid there's even worse news."

"Wait a minute!" Hydro Dude interrupts. "You're saying something other than the word, 'Yes.'"

The doctor nods. "That's precisely my point. I'm afraid I've out-tricked myself. By destroying the letter *B* I've also done away with the word *Bad.*"

"Meaning?"

"Meaning, I can no longer be a Bad Guy. Now, I'm doomed forever and ever to simply be an Bad guy."

"Because there's no *B*?

"You catch on fast."

"But...if you can't be a Bad Guy, how can I save the world?"

"You can't."

"That's terrible. If there are no Bad Guys then all of us superheroes are out of work!"

"Exactly," the doctor agrees. "Unless..."

"Unless what?"

"Unless, you were to accidentally hit this switch on my Gadgetron belt, here, and restore the letter *B* to the world."

"Why can't you do it?"

"Because I'm no longer Bad."

"But I can do it because..."

"Because you're stupid and clumsy."

"Of course." Hydro Dude nods. "Why didn't I think of that?"

"Because you're stupid and clumsy."

"Yes," Hydro Dude nods, "I see your point. Now, let's see, what switch are we talking about?" In a fit of intelligence, Hydro Dude finds the switch labeled:

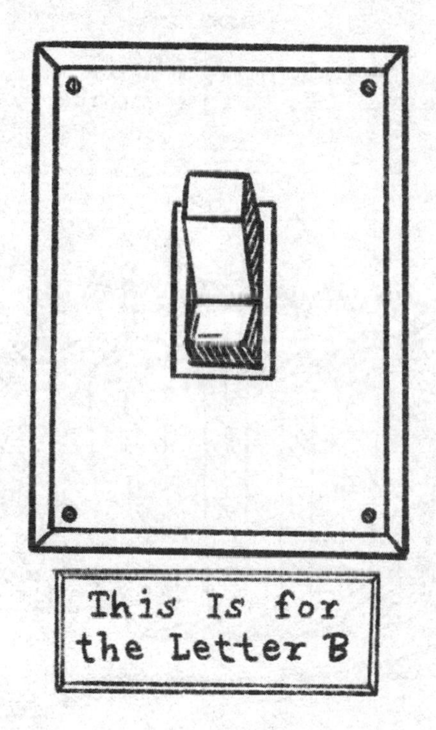

He flips the switch.

There is a loud *SWOOSH* as everything with the letter *B* returns

Bologna,

Bruises,

Brussel sprouts,

Braces,

Bell-bottoms,

Brazil,

Boogers,

Baboons,

Belching.

You name it, it's back, including Backs.

Once again, Hydro Dude has saved the day. Once again, his incredible skills, superhuman strength, and *under*powering intelligence have rescued the world.

Now we can watch ball games, have birthdays, and eat broccoli! (Hey, two out of three ain't bad.)

But, even more importantly, great writers can write great stories with great (and sometimes not so great) superheroes, who are ridding the world of bad guys like Dr. Yes! So stay tuned. I'm afraid there's more where this came from—plenty more.